# Inspector White Tip – A Watcher's Mistake

## The case of the missing Skinny Hind

S. Eden as told by O. Eden

Published by Author Academy Elite
PO Box 43, Powell, OH 43065
www.AuthorAcademyElite.com

Identifiers:
LCCN: 2020916131
ISBN: 978-1-64746-465-3 (paperback)
ISBN: 978-1-6746-466-0 (hardback)
ISBN: 978-1-64746-467-7 (ebook)

Available in paperback, hardback, e-book, and audiobook.

# ACKNOWLEDGEMENTS

This book is dedicated, first and foremost, to my husband. Thank you for spending endless hours reading through my material and keeping me motivated, even when I was being my most stubborn. To our daughter for being the greatest joy in the world and never ceasing to make us proud. To my mum and dad for offering endless support. I love you, and thank you for our Friday night dinners. Friends, who knew I was writing this book, who remained my team of cheerleaders, especially the ones who asked me to write more. To all the children who I have taught for their sheer honesty, empathy and humour. To the memory of my sister, who might be gone, but remains forever in my thoughts, and loved cats - until their fur got everywhere!

Thank you to Oksana Didkova at Kseniyart for Fiverr, for drawing the most beautiful illustrations and listening to every single one of my requests. Each cat was drawn just as I imagined, with the most intricate of details. It was a joy to work with you.

Thank you to Felicity Fox for editing my manuscript to make it the polished masterpiece that it now is. Your words of encouragement and critique were sublime. It has been a pleasure to work with you. Thank you to Tina Morlock for putting me into contact with Felicity and for her editing of the back cover.

Thank you to Nanette O'Neal for the encouragement, especially telling me what you found funny in the manuscript and which ideas you liked.

Thank you to Niccie Kliegl for listening to my initial proposal and telling me the common theme of my work – trust. Following this conversation, I felt I had to write my first book.

Thank you to Kary Oberbrunner for making the whole process accessible and keeping us all motivated.

Thank you to the Nicola Graham and her team at www.reubensretreat.org, who offered support during difficult times. Your work in supporting bereavement is second to none, and invaluable.

Finally, thank you to Oscar, for being the most loyal cat and ensuring that only one other cat comes onto our land. And the other cats in the neighbourhood, for keeping us entertained with your drama.

# CONTENTS

Inspector White Tip

Curly Whiskers

Stripes

Skinny Hind

One Fang

Old Ginger Paws

# 1

## THE MISTAKE

The cat world is an intricate one. Ultimately, it is about being loyal to one's self and making choices about those we choose to have around us. Some cats will sacrifice their own watchers and whisperers for a gain of territory; thus it's hard to find cats to trust.

Almost every cat has a whisperer, a cat who informs them of what's happening in the Neighbourhood. Whisperers sit close to the ground, hiding in the shadows, watching and listening to everything happening. They usually know what the news is before it happens. My whisperer was Curly Whiskers.

Curly was a black cat with the curliest whiskers I'd ever seen. I never asked him how they got like that. I'd be lying if I said that I wasn't curious, but he was good at his job. I didn't question because I didn't need to know. Curly was good enough that I didn't even know he was there until he swiped my legs for fun.

That should have been the first warning. I rarely got things wrong. After all, I was a cat, not a dog. I lost my instincts because it was my first real case. Sit back, as I explain.

Besides a whisperer, almost all cats have a watcher. Watchers usually sat on the rooftops and only went inside when it poured with rain, or they wanted food. To ensure that mine could do the best job, I always made sure she had food. Stripes had humans but spent next to no time with them. She made it her business to watch the world. She slept little and missed even less. Watchers were lean without being skinny and were always the best climbers of the feline world.

Stripes was the best watcher I'd ever known. She chose the tallest spot she could find to allow her to see more of the Neighbourhood. There was little that she didn't see. I'd have trusted her with my tuna. She was the only one who wouldn't eat it. Apart from being a tortoiseshell, she had earned every single one of her markings.

It was six o' clock. I gave Stripes the nod to head down to the roof below. I wasn't nimble enough to make it up to her spot. Besides, I wasn't an informer. I wasn't about to put myself out for something that I didn't have to do.

I dropped the sparrow I'd caught at her feet. Normally she would've devoured it in a couple of bites, but she was cautious. I hissed – she had no reason to question me. That should've been the first warning, but I'm ashamed to say that I was offended. I should've seen that she didn't seem right. She chewed the sparrow, taking much longer between bites. It was almost as though she was thinking about something.

"White Tip, I need you to do me a favour. I need you to find out what happened to Skinny. He's been gone for three days. I think One Fang and his gang have been hanging around. I've seen them heading in that direction. It won't be long until one of them tries to take over," she said.

Stripes was right. One Fang and his gang were thugs. Most were just brawn and only intimidating in numbers. They would've been good fellas if they belonged in other gangs, but that didn't make them forgivable; they made their choice. They knew what One Fang was like.

One Fang was an oversized Persian cat, who was treated to a roast chicken every day. It was the only thing that he said that I actually trusted. There was no way he got that big from cat biscuits. He received his name because he had only one

2

fang left, which he used well against his opponents. Some cats were shaken by his sheer size. He was a boulder, but if they thought about it, they could have easily outrun him. One Fang liked to surprise his opponents by sneaking up on them. He was surprisingly inconspicuous for his size.

It was bad news if he was hanging around. He'd wanted Skinny's land – that was common knowledge. He'd brooded over it for ages. He sat watching his house daily, for hours on end.

I could've been curious about what was so special about Skinny's land, but One Fang didn't interest me. As far as I was concerned, Skinny's land was Skinny's land. That was until he went missing. I should've known that as soon as Skinny went away, One Fang would've been there sniffing around, making it his territory. He'd wanted it for far too long.

There was also a sense of protection that we felt for Skinny Hind. He had already lost one life through heartbreak. His first human had loved him as a kitten, but then he grew up. Kittens don't stay kittens forever. They had doted on him and he used to ride with them in the car, so he never suspected a thing when they shouted him in. Skinny thought he was going on another adventure. They drove for a little bit, and then they pulled up by the pavement, wound down the window, and threw him out of it when they were nowhere near his neighbourhood.

The poor kitten had barely even used his claws. The only thing he'd scratched was his kitten post. He couldn't have been more lost if he'd tried. He looked dishevelled with his fur clung to his ribs. He sat on the pavement for days, in all weathers, waiting for his humans to come back. Curly told him there was no use waiting, but he stayed for a long while. When he realised that there was no point in hoping anymore, he looked like he'd lost another few lives.

It took him ages before he trusted another human again, and even then, it was a surprise that he ever did. Curly took him under his paw and taught him to hunt. It was lucky that the garden they chose was one where the human was fed up with the birds taking over. He wanted some control restored. He fed Skinny every day until the name Skinny no longer made sense. He deserved his land. One Fang and his gang needed to find somewhere else.

I should've heard about Skinny's disappearance from Curly Whiskers. Then, I could tell Stripes what I needed her to look after, but I'd never had a reason before to question her. She usually told me about what she'd seen, kept an eye out for my land, and informed me if there were any intruders. I usually went to her with the jobs, not the other way round.

"Who else knows that he's missing?" I asked.

"Just One Fang and his gang. Be careful. One Fang has been in there several times. He's bound to have the others watching," Stripes warned.

I knew that Stripes was right. One Fang operated with a lot of cats, but he wanted Skinny's land for himself. He had always wanted it for himself and he wasn't about to share with anyone. I looked over at Skinny's land. It looked empty without him. Since he had a human, we saw less of him, but that didn't mean we felt any less protective of him.

One Fang's behaviour irked me. Cats fighting about land wasn't the issue. A cat's got to cat, which means having to fight once in a while to keep or gain territory. It was the way he did it, that got my back up.

Every cat knew that all land was up for grabs except where a cat lived with their human. It was pretty low to think that this land was up for grabs. If a fight occurred here, the Cat Council ruled that the land was restored to its rightful owner, and the trespasser was told to leave. One Fang knew the rule.

There was no confirmation that Skinny was no longer around, yet One Fang seemed to think he could claim the land as though Skinny had never been there. The first thing I needed to do was find out what had happened to Skinny, but if One Fang also got the message to back off, that wasn't a bad thing.

4

# 2

## NOT ON SKINNY'S LAND!

I cautiously made my way over to Skinny's land. I felt a stab of pain in my leg. I should've known it was Curly; I heard him laughing before he revealed himself. There were times when I really wasn't sure whether my wounds would ever heal.

"Do you have to do that every time?" I asked.

"No, but it is fun," Curly laughed.

I licked at the blood. I didn't want One Fang to sniff my scent. I should've known that Curly had worked out where I was heading before I told him. He was a whisperer. It was his job to know. He never questioned why I was heading over in that direction; that was another mistake I made. I should've questioned why Curly wasn't telling me about Skinny. He'd taken him under his paw after all. He was usually one of the first to know if things were awry.

"Don't go for the sparrows; you're there for Skinny," Curly warned.

I instantly felt disappointed. The sparrows would've been a worthwhile treat, but Curly was right. I was there for a job. I suspected that I was in for a fight – One Fang or his gang were bound to be guarding it. There was almost no chance that I'd be able to check the land beforehand for clues as to Skinny's whereabouts, but it was worth a try.

"The house to the right belongs to the Skittle Twins. Make sure you use their land to gain access. They won't do anything; they'll be too scared to fight. Another cat on their land will bowl them over – they're runners," Curly said.

Runners were cats who immediately ran when they saw another cat. They hated fighting. Usually, a lost fight spooked them, or they were pedigree. Humans of pedigrees usually forbid them to fight. If they did, they stayed inside and they learned *not* to fight. Otherwise, they became prisoners. Runners often found themselves compromising themselves: a hierarchy had been established. They knew to make their absence when the other cats appeared. It meant that they shared their land unless they were willing to stand their ground with other cats. Cats usually acted alone, especially on their property. I was intrigued that they came as a pair.

I knew who they were without an introduction when I saw two Siamese cats immediately stand stock-still when they saw me walk towards them. When they realised that I was entering their land, they backed right against the wall until there was nowhere else to go.

"We want no trouble," the left one said.

"You can have it. We'll go back inside," the right one said.

Their submissive nature chilled me. They were so frightened by my presence that they were willing to hand over their land and their fresh air to avoid confrontation. I was cautious. I didn't know who their allies were. I didn't trust them: they would've surrendered to anyone. Who knew what was on the other side of the gate?

"You tell no one I was here, and I'll let you keep your land." I lied, knowing that the Cat Council would give them back their land. It wasn't my fault if other cats didn't keep up with the Neighbourhood rules. Any cat who walked the streets knew that.

The pair of them nodded. I knew they would've done anything that I'd asked of them, but I didn't like that. A cat needed to stand its ground. They deserved their space, free from attack. Their land was their safe space, or it should've been.

I walked past them and under the gate. I wanted to run away from them and wondered whether they ever used that powerful strategy – tackling fear with fear – probably not because they'd already disappeared before the other cat came close. True to their nature, they backed off and hid under the car. I breathed a sigh of relief, until I saw Old Ginger Paws dozing in the grass. They could've told me he was there. I realised that they probably wanted to get away as soon as possible.

Old Ginger Paws annoyed me nearly as much as One Fang. It was no surprise to me that they worked together. He arrived in the Neighbourhood not long after me.

Whenever a cat moves to a new neighbourhood, it takes them a while to establish themselves. Cats have to have a lot of fights – it's the way to acquire more land than only their human's territory. It was much smarter to do this because it meant eating more meals and having more shelter in bad weather if their original human was missing. It was also nice to choose when some of the meals were getting a bit *samey*.

Sometimes, when a land hasn't ever had a cat with a human before, the other cats claim it and can be stubborn about giving it up. Usually, the humans intervene for this though, and the fights occur because they were offended about losing territory.

When I arrived in the Neighbourhood, I fought several times a day. The Duchess, my human, often bathed my scratches, but she understood that a cat's got to cat. The Male One was soft and even thought of keeping me inside to protect me, but that would've been worse. I would've had to start over again. Within a couple of days, I had a tonne of scratches, but more importantly, I'd won the land.

Old Ginger Paws made the catastrophic mistake of coming onto my humans' land. I would've accepted that, if he hadn't persisted on coming over. He understood the first time my human was home and left when I told him. When he returned, I chased him off. The third time, I made sure he knew my humans included the surrounding houses. I made sure he didn't return.

It was no shock to me when he suddenly, Old Ginger Paws and One Fang and his gang were spotted together. I had a whisperer and an informer. He needed these too, but he also needed the back up of One Fang. Old Ginger Paws was large and lazy. His fighting skills – or lack of – meant that there was no way he would acquire any land, which was where One Fang came in.

One Fang had too much land. He had enough that he couldn't watch over it, or so he claimed. Suddenly, Old Ginger Paws seemed to take the west side of One Fang's territory. I was never sure of whether I believed One Fang handed it over or Old Ginger Paws won it. But it made no difference to me – I wanted Old Ginger Paws gone from my land, and he was.

I trotted past. It was easy. Old Ginger Paws snored away. I scaled the fence. Some guard he was, when he slept on the job.

The minute I landed, I realised how well Skinny had done for himself. The garden was a cat's paradise. He was onto a gold mine. His humans had a pond filled with fish. It had a net, but it looked easy enough to pull the fish out of. I was surprised there were fish swimming there and that hadn't been eaten by the cats. I was tempted to take one, but as I was there for work, I knew that I couldn't.

I soon came across the sparrow's nest that Curly had warned me about. I watched their naivety with admiration. The mother sparrow fed her babies with her back turned to the world, which made her the perfect catch. I sat in the shade and watched the mother sparrow's head turning to each of her children. There were just enough of them to be pretty without running amok. That was when I was blind-sided.

Before I could move, pain shot through my neck. I knew who it was before I caught sight of him – One Fang. I made sure that I put my new, freshly sharpened claws to the test as I sunk my back claws into him. He released me instantly. So, I took my chance to then spin and sink my claws into his face. Blood dyed his white fur a crimson red.

When he flinched, I knew he was an amateur fighter. He relied on shocking his opponents, and they fell for it. One Fang was one of the worst fighters I'd ever known. His weakness was that he wasn't a good fighter, but he didn't want anyone else to know that, so he made sure he took the first shot. He'd never been challenged before. I made sure that he knew I loathed bullies.

I went straight to his weakness; I had all my teeth and gnashed them together. I could've bitten him, but I'd just eaten. I didn't want that bad taste in my mouth. I'd save that move in case I really needed it. One Fang backed away with a look of genuine shock. Temporarily, I forgot that Old Ginger Paws was in the Skittle Twins garden until I saw him stumbling over the fence. One Fang sneered.

"This is ours now!" One Fang claimed.

I yawned in his face at the sight of two of them. He'd persuaded a runner to help him because he needed a whole gang of cats to start a revolution. It was laughable. I arched my back, a move known to scare a dog or two. I didn't make it a regular thing to fight with dogs, but sometimes they needed a reminder that I didn't like them, and no, they couldn't wander onto my land. Any marks they made were in vain on my territory. I wanted those two cats to know that Skinny's land was mine until he returned.

Old Ginger Paws looked to One Fang for back up. I knew he was terrified. He'd lost one fight to me and he didn't want to lose another. One Fang looked back sternly. If he was prepared to have him defeated, I wondered who else he was prepared to sacrifice.

"I'm not fighting him. If you want to fight me One Fang, then you fight me," I warned.

One Fang was furious. He wanted me to believe that he was strong and fierce, but he was neither. He knew it, and so did I. He wanted Old Ginger Paws as a shield. I saw Old Ginger Paws wanted to act, but he couldn't. The cat had his tongue, and his paws, it seemed.

Fortunately for him, we had been so busy fighting that none of us noticed Skinny's human until we were all soaked; he'd turned the hose on us. I hated water, but made sure I was the last to leave because I knew exactly where my next destination was going to be.

The Skittle Twins forgot themselves for a minute and laughed when they saw that I was soaked from head to toe. I swiped at the left one, who banged heads with the right. They clinked so loudly; I was surprised that there was anything in their heads. But, they sat up.

I could've questioned the Skittle Twins about why they hadn't told me about Old Ginger Paws being on their land, but I saw that I would've only have been asking for my own pride. I knew why they couldn't talk; they were afraid of One Fang and petrified of what might happen to them. The fear was so raw and real; it stopped them from really living. My pride wanted to question them until they were more afraid of me than One Fang, but what would that have done for me? Their fear made them untrustworthy and unreliable. I didn't need cats like that feeding me tuna, telling me things that I wanted to hear and remaining silent during my anger. I knew that I just had to chalk it up to experience. They couldn't be trusted.

Out of the corner of my eye, I saw something that shook me to my core. Shivers ran through my spine and my hair stood on end. The Skittle Twins scampered fast. They must have thought that I was coming for them, but they were wrong. This was much bigger than either of them or their actions.

My tail widened, and my back arched. I realised that there was no way that Stripes could see Skinny's land, not even from her roof top. A lower, protruding wall, three houses down blocked her view. His land was in her blind spot. I could have kicked myself. There was no way that I could've known that before; I couldn't climb that high. She'd always jumped down for me.

It'd never crossed my mind that Stripes would ever lie to me. Besides Curly Whiskers, she was the most honest cat I'd ever known. She was my watcher, and I had to be able to trust her. I realised that someone must have tipped her off about Skinny Hind. Though I could accept that, I needed to know who it was. She'd compromised all three of us.

At first, I wanted to question Stripes, but then I knew that she'd be defensive when I did. She would've asked questions like, why didn't I trust her? But I did trust her. She just hadn't shared all of the tuna with me. It wasn't like her. She usually told me everything.

I headed towards Curly Whiskers. He never questioned why I went towards Skinny's land. He had to know Skinny was missing. Whisperers knew about everything going on in the Neighbourhood. They sifted through all of the tuna, until it came to the crucial tuna. He had to know who'd spoken to Stripes.

The problem with whisperers was that they were hard to find. They had a knack of only appearing when they wanted to talk. I knew why that was. They had to keep their ears close to the ground to know everything that was going on. If they were constantly talking, they'd never be able to listen. Obviously I didn't want to call him because that would've been foolish. It would've tipped another whisperer off that I was looking for something, which got cats into a lot of trouble.

First and foremost, cats are suspicious and assume intruders will try to steal their land, which causes agitation and more fights. They don't think rationally, and suddenly, they could fight anyone and everyone. Secondly, the fighting would've meant that I wasn't focused on the task at hand, which was to find out what had happened to Skinny and why Stripes wanted it investigated. Thirdly, it meant that notorious cat gangs were aware of something and would use it as leverage to gain more land.

The good thing about Curly Whiskers was that he was never too far away. As soon as he saw the white tip of my tail, he sought me out, without being spotted.

I headed over to my eight o'clock cuddles whilst I waited, feeling sorry for myself. I was still dripping wet. Sure enough, there was a bowl of biscuits waiting for me on the doorstep. I made sure that I made my voice heard before tucking in, being I was too cold to enjoy them anyway. I heard the footsteps coming to the backdoor.

"Oh dear!" The human said when he saw me.

The human welcomed me in like a king. My eight o'clock cuddles were my second family. There were so many of them, that I never missed out on anything. Sometimes, I even got second or third helpings of cat biscuits, especially if the older ones were in other rooms when I arrived. They fussed and cooed over me for hours. It was marvellous during winter or on rainy nights when I wanted to be inside.

After a while though, the constant attention was claustrophobic, and it began to irritate me, so that was when I chose to leave. Then, I went back to the Duchess and my first family. I liked that I still got some fuss and that I was allowed to just sleep without fuss or interruptions.

That night was different though. I felt myself starting to develop a cold, so I needed someone to fuss and look after me.

The old lady had my blanket ready. I made sure that I milked it for more than it was worth. I meowed sadly. The child fetched a towel for me and dried me off. Then, he lifted me onto my blanket. The old lady wrapped me up in my blanket and smoothed my fur. The teenager fed me my biscuits. I needed to make sure that I didn't overdo it though: I didn't want a trip to the vets. I wasn't *that* ill.

When I'd napped a little, I made sure that I thanked each of them for my care. I rubbed my head against each of them, then sat by the sliding doors. They knew the call. I meowed as I left.

Curly waited for me. I felt the familiar swipe at my legs before I saw his eyes appear. Against the night, I felt like I was talking to just his eyes. Black cats made the best whisperers because they were harder to spot. The only trouble was if they lived with humans, they usually had to stay inside at night and roam in the day. Day time was the worst time to roam. Cats want to be out at night when there is more range to hunt. Luckily for me, Curly's home was the streets.

"You need to cross the road quickly; the Cat Council has a search warrant for you!" Curly warned. "I'll be over in the morning."

I scampered quickly before I was hunted.

# 3

# THE POWERS OF ONE FANG

The Cat Council was usually made up of cats that had lived in the Neighbourhood for the longest time. They were usually inconspicuous because they didn't want to be bothered with all of the Neighbourhood issues. Cats were supposed to sort their own battles. However, the Cat Council was able to issue locked-in orders.

Locked-in orders could be for hours, days, weeks, or forever. Cats weren't allowed to exit their human land until they completed the order. They were under constant surveillance by the Cat Council. If they broke the order, cats were exiled from the Neighbourhood, not even allowed on their human land. They were chased by cats in the Neighbourhood until they were well over the border and usually too frightened and outnumbered to return.

I only knew of one cat who was issued a locked-in order. His name was Lion Paw, a large cat who belonged to one of the notorious cat gangs. No cat could fight him. He had to be locked in to give the other cats a chance. Many went to the vet for their injuries, and no other cats could fight him. His lock-in allowed other cats a chance. Lion Paw was so big that even if he'd have broken the order, he probably could've taken every cat that chased him and won. Lion Paw was decent enough to accept his order, usually when he wanted a long sleep. There was a rumour that he was the reason why One Fang only had one tooth left. I didn't want to be the second cat who received one.

The Duchess was pleased to see me and didn't ask questions. She accepted that I was home. As I said, a little bit of fuss, the Duchess made a little bit of fuss but then left me alone. I wanted to be alone and curled up on my bed, away from the window. There was bound to be another whisperer or watcher who saw me. I didn't want to witness my own demise or let another cat watch me. After my nap, I wanted to put together all of the clues that'd brought me there. If Curly said he was going to speak to me in the morning, there was no use in worrying about it, especially when I'd already lost three hours of proper sleep. My nap at my eight o'clock cuddles just didn't cover it, so I curled up in a tight ball.

When I woke up, I almost forgot about the Cat Council, until I saw a cat sitting at the window. I was enraged when I saw Old Ginger Paws there. There was no way that he was a part of the Cat Council. He had lived in the Neighbourhood for less time than me! If he was, then something had gone badly wrong. I clenched my teeth together as I made my way to the window. Who did he think he was sitting on my window sill? The sun hadn't even risen in the sky!

Even if I had wanted to, there was no way that I could run Old Ginger Paws off my land; my humans were sleeping. I had to grit my teeth. I jumped down from the window and went back to my bed. He pawed at the window. Maybe it was to get my attention; perhaps it was to provoke me, but I turned around to show him that I wasn't interested.

"White Tip, I need you to come to the window before the Cat Council sees me," Old Ginger Paws said.

I knew that the whisperers and watchers would've shared the tuna of my warrant with their posse. They had a duty to inform the Cat Council if they saw me. The humiliation came from Old Ginger Paws seeking me out as soon as he found out. I had no interest in what he had to say to me, but I knew that he wasn't going to leave soon. I made sure that I stretched my legs first. I wasn't about to hurry for him.

"They have got Stripes," Old Ginger Paws said.

I was sceptical. Stripes never spoke to Old Ginger Paws out of choice. She thought he was as cunning as I did. Stripes stayed at a higher elevation unless she was sharing tuna with me. I wasn't even sure that Old Ginger Paws actually knew her name. There was no reason for him to know. Stripes never came onto the ground. She lived on her roof watching the world. For the entire time I'd lived in the Neighbourhood, I always took a find up to her. Stripes didn't care for humans. She liked her freedom and chose to leave her humans behind as soon as she ventured outdoors. I'd never asked her why and I never needed to know, but I regretted not asking more questions.

"Where have they taken her?" I asked.

"I don't know, I just wanted you to know that they have her," he said.

I was protective of Stripes. She was my watcher. She informed me of things and generally kept me out of trouble. Because of her, I was prepared for every fight and had a large territory because she made sure that I knew when land was vacated. And I brought her food from my land or hunting. I wasn't really sure that she could fight. She was an avid climber with little need for her to be on the ground. Everything she wanted was on the roof. She even had a make-shift shelter for when the weather was really bad. If she'd been arrested, I wasn't sure that she'd be able to handle being away from her spot.

I was also wary that this was a ploy to ensure that I was issued a locked-in order and then exiled from the Neighbourhood. I knew that the Cat Council wanted to see me, but it was still best that I waited until Curly came back to me and confirmed whether I needed to face them or that he had sorted it all out.

The Cat Council had the best deterrent with one of their guards, Pomeranian's Friend.

Pomeranian's Friend was known for being a feral cat. No one wanted to be within his company for long. His fur was so flea-ridden, he no longer reacted when they bit him. He had worms, ticks; you name it. He was named Pomeranian's Friend because he ate anything he found. He scooted across the floor regularly. It didn't matter how long the food had been there. If he saw it, he ate it. He had no standards. He refused to hunt and scavenged off the leftovers of the other cats. I didn't want him chaperoning me anywhere. He might have been feral, but he never needed to fight. His appearance was enough of a deterrent. He was fairly well-natured, for a feral cat.

He sat on my land all night. Other cats were allowed to come and go, but he was there to make sure that I didn't escape. I knew I had to have done something bad if he was there to watch me.

"I have no way out yet," I said, looking at Pomeranian's Friend. "I'll have to wait for my humans to unlock the door."

Old Ginger Paws nodded as though he understood. I wasn't sure if he wanted to help: I was never sure whether he was genuine. He had no reason to be. His loyalties were with One Fang. I had to give it to him; he was a brilliant actor. He jumped down and jumped over the fence, so that I could see him leave.

I hated him for planting the seed of doubt. It left me worrying about Stripes, even though there was little I could do to help. Curly Whiskers was bound to know more than me. Still, I worried that she was okay. I curled up in a ball in my bed and prayed Curly came before my humans woke. The last thing I wanted was for the Male One to throw me outside because he thought it was good for me. He didn't understand. The Duchess let me decide. I hoped it was she who walked down the stairs. I had a terrible nap, fretting about what was going to happen. I only slept for another four hours.

When the Duchess came into my room, I breathed a sigh of relief. She wasn't going to get me into more trouble. She fed me and let me be. I thought that Curly would've visited me. Then, I worried that the Cat Council had arrested him too. The waiting was frustrating, and I had no idea how long it'd be. I knew that I could trust him; there was no doubt that he'd intended to pass on the message. I knew that he was supposed to have been by to see me, so his absence meant bad news.

When the Male One entered the room, I did my best to hiss when he opened the door. Of course, he didn't get the message. He was going to have me arrested! I made sure he knew how angry I was by scratching and biting at his hand. I sunk my teeth in until I could taste his blood, then I ran under the table. I sank my claws into the carpet. The Male One got the message. I didn't feel bad. He had no idea what was happening. I hated it when he decided to send me outside, so I made it clear when I wanted my freedom. Silly human!

As time passed slowly, it was only making me more stir crazy. In the end, I had to stand at the door. I'd waited too long for Curly to show his face. He'd never kept me waiting for so long before. Something had to have happened to him! I paced by the window again and again.

By the time Curly Whiskers arrived, I was frantic. Big clumps of my fur fell out, and I only managed to eat most of my food. It was almost a waste.

"Sorry I didn't come sooner; the guards are everywhere," Curly explained. Pomeranian's Friend had left in the morning.

I knew that there had to be a good reason for why Curly hadn't come sooner. I nodded my appreciation.

"What did you actually do to One Fang?" Curly asked.

"It's more like what did he do to me. He bit me, so I dug my claws in," I said.

"The Council have made it clear that you have to be tried for unreasonable force and treason," Curly said.

My jaw dropped. How was it that One Fang could take his opponents by surprise, but they could not retaliate? The world suddenly felt like a very unjust place.

"He's had hours to build supporters, and he has a witness," Curly said.

I thought for a moment whilst I processed the tuna. A witness? Then, I remembered Old Ginger Paws. I could've yowled at the injustice, but I didn't want to alert the humans that I was in trouble. They were bound to assume that Curly was an enemy there for a fight. I didn't want him to be chased off my land.

There were two options, I realised. Option one was to wait it out until the fuss died down. Sure, that was credible, except the not knowing was driving me slowly insane. I needed to know properly what was going on. Option two was to face the Council. I gulped. They had the power to enforce a lock-in for goodness knows how long, but at least I knew for myself. I could hear it first-hand, which was always the best way to hear news.

"What about Stripes? Have they taken her?" I asked.

"She hasn't been up there for a while," Curly replied.

After being sanctioned for one night, I was ready to hear my fate, even if it was only for my freedom to walk to and from the Council. I could not bear not knowing whether or not Stripes was okay. It sounded as though Old Ginger Paws was right. I needed to find out where she was. She was bound to be at the trial. Then, I'd have an answer.

I called the Male One to the door. Of course, he was slow to react. He was playing martyr to having been hurt. He never regarded my feelings or thought about why I had to attack him. Sometimes, he really infuriated me. He asked whether or not I was sorry. I'm a cat – probably not. After the lecture, I was ready to face whatever the Council had in store for me.

Jet

Ebony

# 4

## THE CAT COUNCIL

When I stepped outside, the fresh air immediately made me feel better about my decision. Hiding away forever would've been stupid, especially as I would've been the one imprisoning myself. I wasn't a runner; I faced my problems.

I sank my claws into the shed. It'd been several hours. I wanted to look sharp before the Council and thought they could do with a proper sharpening. The Male One popped his head out and shouted at me to stop doing that. I wanted to hiss, but I didn't want him to be outside for much longer, or he might have made me go back inside, which was something I really didn't want. I took my claws out and then took the time to give myself a proper clean up.

As soon as I reached the front driveway, my paws hadn't touched the ground for a second, when I saw them waiting for me. Two black cats, Jet and Ebony, strut forwards.

I'd seen Jet around the Neighbourhood. She usually slept on the bonnet of her human's car and never seemed to do an awful lot. She always seemed to only laze about in the sun. So, I was a little shocked to see her there. Her street was around the corner, and I didn't really care for the number of dogs that seemed to live there – I'd rather her than me.

I knew *of* Ebony, but knew very little *about* him. He often hid under cars. I supposed that he was a whisperer. He kept himself well-hidden, rarely visible around the Neighbourhood.

"Inspector White Tip?" Jet asked.

"Yes," I said.

"By order of the Council, you are summoned to a hearing for unreasonable force and treason," Ebony said. "You must walk with us."

As soon as he spoke, I saw cats coming from every direction under cars, garden fences and walls. I had no idea whether they were chaperons or spectators, but neither felt better. I wasn't about to run anywhere, so their presence had the desired effect. I walked with my head held high.

I could've bowed it, but that would have given the impression that I was guilty. I was the victim of fiction, and the shame wasn't my burden. I hoped One Fang had strong enough conviction to tell his story. I was almost keen to hear his version of events, especially as I was being charged with unreasonable force and treason. I knew that there must have been lots of twists and turns. I'd known cats who've done way worse, and the Council stayed well clear.

The treason part was the most alarming. I knew that Skinny Hind wasn't on the Cat Council, so maybe that meant One Fang was. I was almost sure that he wasn't, although he could've been. He was a pedigree cat and had been in the Neighbourhood for a long time, so it was possible. He didn't conduct himself like a member of the Cat Council though. He broke many rules and quite often challenged cats for land, even when it was their human's land.

I started to search for Stripes' face amongst the crowd. I began to feel really anxious. I hadn't seen her since the fight. She was bound to know that I'd been summoned – it was her job as a watcher. It was her job to know what was happening in the Neighbourhood. When I didn't see her, I started to feel a little embarrassed and put my head down then.

By the time I arrived at the Council's meeting point, I felt disappointed. I should've had the support of my watcher. If she wasn't there, it meant that I didn't know her at all. I'd spent a lot of time looking for cats that I could trust.

It wasn't a long walk, but it was a treacherous one. Imagine, having everyone looking at you, assuming you are guilty before proven innocent. It wasn't fair. I hadn't done anything wrong. Cats could be a judgmental bunch. It didn't take much for them to condemn others.

"Mind your head," Jet warned.

I looked up at the wrong moment. It would've been better if she hadn't said anything because I banged my head on the entrance and realised that I was at a burrow. It knocked the breath out of me for a moment. That would leave a lump.

"What are we stopping for, a bite to eat?" I asked as I rubbed the top of my head.

"It's been abandoned for a while," She explained, rolling her eyes.

I wasn't sure what I thought of her. It was as though I was wasting her time. I never asked for the trial. If she was angry at anyone, it should've been One Fang.

I followed Jet and Ebony into the burrow. It was roomy for a burrow. I expected it to be small, especially if it was for a warren of rabbits. Of course, there were all sorts of tunnels, but I was still surprised by how big the place was. It had to span the entire underground of the Neighbourhood. Some of the cats must've opened up the space. This was the work of something more than a rabbit. It was more like a den than a warren. I supposed the pedigrees wouldn't know the difference. They didn't go out into the wild much.

Five cats sat at the top: a Bengal, a Ragdoll, a British short hair, Jet, and Ebony. They sat on a high bench, looking down at us all. I was invited to sit on a stand next to the bench, which looked out at the audience. I knew I was on trial. It didn't feel comfortable.

I looked into the gallery. Stripes wasn't there. Curly Whiskers, my loyal whisperer and friend, sat at the front. His green eyes shone, I was pleased to have him there. It made me feel less alone.

"Inspector White Tip of Crescent Drive?" The Bengal asked.

I nodded respectfully. Suddenly, it began to feel overwhelming. I realised that it could be my last day of freedom.

"Inspector White Tip, you are charged with unreasonable force and treason on a Mr One Fang. I understand that the events took place on Skinny Hind's territory."

My mouth was dry. It suddenly felt incredibly real. I'd never been a cat to sit in the gallery. I usually had greater interests to investigate. I was surprised by the turn out. I had no idea that so many cats took an interest.

"It's unusual to have to close the doors to the gallery, but this case has drawn unbelievable interest. I suspect this might have to do with the act of treason that commenced," the Bengal continued.

Treason! I never committed an act of treason. I hated hearing it again. It still made me angry.

I still couldn't believe that I never knew that One Fang was a member of the Council. I wrongly assumed that a cat like One Fang would have bragged about his title and prestige. He usually bragged about everything else. He had a lot of bravado. Also, how hadn't he gained Skinny's land? If he was on the Council, he could have almost anything that he wanted. But this was more than a tale. I was in a lot of hot water. My mouth went as dry a desert.

"Mr One Fang, do you care to step forward?" the Ragdoll asked, looking into the gallery.

In all of the excitement, I hadn't clocked that One Fang or Old Ginger Paws had even arrived. Suddenly, I questioned whether I should've even bothered being an inspector. It was my job to see things that other cats missed. I should've been looking out for him as soon as I arrived, yet I was more bothered about seeing Curly and Stripes. I had to be far more objective than that.

"I'm afraid Mr One Fang felt too threatened to step forward. Instead, he asked me to speak for him. My name is Brown Crown," he said.

Afraid! There was no chance that One Fang was too afraid to come to the trial. I was surprised that he wanted any cat knowing that. He usually liked to intimidate the other cats. This had to be another cat's idea. I knew that One Fang would've taken far more convincing than that. I'd never seen Brown Crown before. He was an all-white cat except for a brown head and brown ears. It was a fitting name. He looked pretty petite to be from One Fang's gang. It was probably his idea for One Fang to stay away. He must be one charismatic cat to convince him that it was better for him to pretend that he was too fearful of attending the trial. It made him look weak. Other cats would assume that they could use this against him. It wasn't a wise move to make.

"Mr Crown, this is most unusual. Do you have the list of witnesses?" the Bengal asked.

A list? I thought there was only one. Curly had told me that there was only one. I knew about Old Ginger Paws and was curious to know who the other was. I looked at Curly. We locked eyes in a stare. I knew that he was telling me to relax, without telling anyone else. He wasn't expecting there to be any other witnesses either.

"I do. All four have agreed to testify," Brown Crown said.

Four? How were there four witnesses? The only cats who were there were One Fang and Old Ginger Paws. The others had to be lying.

"Thank you. Please take the floor," the Bengal said.

Brown Crown walked forwards. I had to hand it to One Fang. The story was starting to look credible. I hoped that they were able to pick holes in the statement.

"Mr One Fang claims that he was concerned for the welfare of his loyal friend, Skinny Hind. He watched Inspector White Tip enter via the Skittle Twins property. He entered the land through the gate on Skinny Hind's land to find Inspector White Tip poaching sparrows. When he asked him to leave, Inspector White Tip became aggressive, bit One Fang and clawed his paws. He attempted to attack Mr Ginger Paws, but failed," Brown Crown said.

I was so angry that I could have hissed, but shouting out wouldn't to do me any favours. They'd painted me to be aggressive, so I had to do my utmost to remain calm and poised. My opportunity to speak would come later. I had to listen to everything that was said about me to enable me to pick holes in their statement.

"Inspector White Tip, were you aware that the land was occupied?" the British Short Hair asked.

"Yes, I'm very…" I started.

"That's all we need to know," the British Short Hair interrupted.

I had to ensure that my answers were well-thought and concise. That cat was never going to let me speak properly. I was going to look awful if I wasn't careful.

"The statement mentioned one act of treason. Does this need to be amended to two charges?" The Bengal asked.

Brown Crown looked to the gallery. I followed his gaze and made sure that I reached the Skittle Twins' gaze and burned them with my glare. Fortunately, one of them looked at me and convinced the other. They both shook their heads.

"No, they are happy for there to be only charge," Brown Crown confirmed.

Who knew that those two were members of the Council? At first, I was livid. I thought they should've forewarned me, but then they were afraid. They felt ambushed. Does any cat think within reason when they feel scared? Besides, there were a couple of tricks I had hidden within my fur.

"Very well," the Bengal replied. "Proceed."

"Mr Ginger Paws asked Inspector White Tip to leave, and at that point, he left. Upon leaving Skinny Hind's land, Inspector White Tip had an altercation with the Skittle Twins before leaving for his territory," Brown Crown said.

"Inspector White Tip, do you agree with the statement?" the Ragdoll asked.

"Parts," I said. I made sure that I kept myself precise. I didn't want to be backed into the corner again on a mishap of speech.

"Which parts don't you agree on?" the Ragdoll asked.

"The Skittle Twins gave me their permission and even offered me their land, and I gave it back to them, so long as they remained silent about me being there. They broke their agreement by informing One Fang that I was there. When I entered their land, Old Ginger Paws lay there sleeping, so he committed treason. Stripes asked me to investigate the land to investigate where Skinny Hind was. It's been known for some time that One Fang has wanted Skinny Hind's land, but no one knew why.

When I arrived, I saw for myself why a cat would be in awe of the land: there's a pond and, of course, a wealth of birds to hunt. I would be lying if I told you that I never once looked at the sparrows, but I was there for my job, to investigate. As my mind was distracted, One Fang bit me, and then I had to defend myself. I never really got a chance to fight with Old Ginger Paws because Skinny's human sprayed us with a hose. I'm here today, and you'll see his tooth mark on my neck," I explained.

The Bengal nodded at Jet and Ebony, who walked forwards. Ebony parted my fur and nodded at the bench. I realised that One Fang, or Brown Crown, must have known that he would've been caught.

"Skittle Left, what state was Inspector White Tip's fur when you found him?" the Short hair asked.

"It was dry…I mean wet, I think." Skittle Left replied.

Suddenly, I felt the tension rise in the room. I knew what was happening. Skittle Left had been instructed what to say, and One Fang had sent his witnesses to make sure that he said it.

"Thank you Skittle Left. Skittle Right, did you forfeit your land and receive it back for a secret?" the Short Hair asked.

Skittle Right looked to the ground. She knew that I was telling the truth, but the only thing she could do was stare at the ground whilst she shook her head. I hoped that the bench knew that she was lying. They had to know both of the Skittle Twins – they were part of the Council.

"Do you accept that Inspector White Tip couldn't have committed treason?" the Bengal continued. "Otherwise, this would be a street fight, and we'd have no reason to question Inspector White Tip."

Skittle Right continued to stare at her paws as she nodded her head. I wanted to jump down and demand that she looked the members of the bench in the eye as she responded, but it was no use. The Cat Council was untouchable, no matter how unreasonable they were. Their word had higher status than anyone else's. It was a good job that One Fang wasn't a member of the Council. That at least assured me.

"Thank you. Mr Ginger Paws, can you step forward?" the Bengal asked.

Old Ginger Paws took his sweet time to stand before the bench. He'd groomed in an attempt to appear as a respectful cat. He looked solemn.

"Mr Ginger Paws, were you on the land of the Skittle Twins?" the Ragdoll asked.

"Yes. They granted their permission for me to stand on land," Old Ginger Paws replied.

"Why would they do that?" the Bengal asked.

"I wanted to rest," Old Ginger Paws said. I saw that he was starting to worry because he hadn't thought about being

29

asked that question. Clearly, Brown Crown hadn't prepared him for that.

"Could you not have rested on your own land?" the Bengal asked.

"Their land is warm and helps me sleep better. Mine has gravel throughout with no furniture," he said.

"How did you find yourself on Skinny Hind's land?" the Ragdoll asked.

"I heard a cat in trouble, and when I arrived on the scene, White Tip had sunk his claws into One Fang's paws," he said.

"Which direction was Inspector White Tip in relation to Mr One Fang?" the Ragdoll asked.

"He was face to face," Old Ginger Paw said.

"There is a charge of unreasonable force. As far as I can see, it was a cat fight with Inspector White Tip showing a bite mark of one tooth on his neck. It sounds perfectly reasonable for a cat to defend themselves when bitten by another," the Bengal said.

"What was the state of your fur when you left the property?" the Bengal asked.

"W…dry," Old Ginger Paws said.

I was pleased that the Council had started to make Old Ginger Paws sweat. He deserved it for lying about me.

"Thank you," the Bengal said. "Who is our fourth witness?"

"Ms Stripes has agreed to testify," Brown Crown said.

Jet and Ebony left to summon her into the room.

My heart thumped in my chest. How had they managed to get Stripes to testify? Most cats were unable to climb up to her look out spot because it was so high.

I started to make connections quickly. When Old Ginger Paws came to visit me, they'd already taken Stripes. She would've been scared because she never needed to fight. She must've been intimidated by One Fang's cats to get me to investigate Skinny's disappearance. I saw no other way. How else would she know about Skinny Hind's land when it was in her blind spot? She rarely stepped down from her post. She only spoke to me. Curly stayed close to the ground to hear what was going on. I was the go-between. It was the way we worked.

When I arrived in the Neighbourhood, it took me a long time to get Stripes to work with me. I had no idea she was there, until I was tracking birds flying overhead. They flew past and she snatched one with her paws. I went back daily to ask her to work with me. She ignored me for months because she wanted no part in the Neighbourhood. I had to show her that I wasn't part of any gang. She wanted no part in a cat gang.

The only reason why Stripes agreed to work with me was when she witnessed Skinny Hind being dropped by his humans, even though it was streets away. When I saw him walking the streets, she begged me not to fight him. She wanted me to protect him. She believed that every cat had a right to at least one space of their own. I agreed to protect him for a while, on the agreement that she would be my watcher. It was then that she decided to be in a trio with Curly Whiskers and me.

Stripes came into the room. She looked dishevelled but fierce. I felt guilty that she'd been taken and put into danger. I saw One Fang's gang had tested her. I hoped that they hadn't managed to chip at our trust. Unfortunately, working as a watcher or whisperer, or with any role in the Neighbourhood, meant we were susceptible to being attacked for tuna. There was always a risk.

"Ms Stripes can you confirm the state of each cat's fur when they left Skinny Hind's land?" the Ragdoll asked.

"It was soaking wet," Stripes confirmed.

"How did Inspector White Tip learn about the disappearance of Skinny Hind?" the Ragdoll continued.

"I told him myself. He was one of the cats that we looked out for. He had been abandoned by one set of humans. We made it our business to look out for him," Stripes said.

"Has Skinny Hind returned to his land?" the Ragdoll asked.

"No," Stripes replied.

"When did you notice that he'd disappeared?" the Short Hair asked.

"I saw his humans carrying him to the car with a sheet over him, four days ago," Stripes said.

Conversation erupted around the room.

# 5

## DEAD OR ALIVE?

The world seemed to stop for a minute. Whenever I got sad news, the world stopped. Stripes had kept the tuna from me, and I understood why. She wanted me to find answers. She knew that it'd hurt me to know that he was carried out covered by a blanket. The chances of him being alive were slim. Emotions stopped me from reasoning. An inspector has to be rational at all times. Emotions hinder their work.

White noise followed. I looked around the room. Their mouths were moving, but no sound was connected. It was like I was frozen in time. My stomach churned.

It was the first time that I'd seen Curly look sad. He looked more than sad. He was devastated. The thought of his prodigy having died, was unthinkable.

The first noise I heard was the claw of the Bengal as she scraped it across the bench. It made everyone stand to attention.

"Does this mean that Skinny Hind is dead?" the Bengal asked.

"I don't know," Stripes answered. There was a lump in her throat.

I knew if pressed, she would've said what she really thought. Everyone thought it. If Skinny had been taken to the vets alive, someone would've had to carry him out in a crate. With a blanket, the prognosis wasn't good. However, he'd travelled in the car with his previous humans, which meant they'd trusted him not to run. I wasn't ready to give up hope just yet.

Curly coughed. It wasn't like him. He was normally inconspicuous. I looked in his direction. He narrowed his eyes at Stripes. Normally, I would've hissed at him. We were a trio. Sure, he didn't speak to Stripes often because he needed to stay close to the ground, but if I trusted her, he needed to. The minute that one of us questioned the other, was the minute that the trust was gone.

Curly's head turned. Stripes was looking in that direction too. Something wasn't right. I couldn't properly make out who they were looking at. Then, I clocked the cat that they were staring at: a tawny coloured cat scratching at the seat. He then shifted along the floor, edging closer towards the Skittle Twins. Of course, the Skittle Twins would never make a fuss. They were far too scared for that.

"Why did it matter to you that Skinny Hind was missing?" the Short Hair asked.

The Short Hair started to irritate me. There was the news that Skinny Hind might be dead, yet he showed no mercy. I knew he was the sort of cat who didn't have a whisperer or watcher because he betrayed them. I didn't like his style. It started to irk me.

"Skinny is a part of the Neighbourhood. I saw him thrown from his human's car," Stripes said. "It took him a long time to be taken in by his new humans."

"If Skinny Hind is declared to be dead, it'll mean his land will be up for tenancy," the Bengal said. "We now must discuss the events in light of all of the tuna."

I made sure to remain sat on the stand. No cat should be aware that Curly Whiskers or Stripes worked with me. Some of One Fang's cats had already gotten to Stripes, which I knew was unpleasant. I didn't want Curly Whiskers exposed to that too, so I remained stoic on the stand and avoided direct eye contact. Stripes jumped down and joined the cats in the gallery. I was pleased that she didn't sit close to Curly.

I looked towards the Skittle Twins. They of course looked uncomfortable, but those two were uncomfortable in their own skin. They probably wanted to be the first to leave, but that was impossible when the bench was in discussion. All eyes would be on them. Even if they tried to hide in the crowd, the mistake they made was that they were forever in each other's company. They were easy to identify, even in a crowd. Cats didn't hang around all the time in the company of other cats. Even those that lived with humans forced to accept another feline's company eventually got fed up with each other. Most cats felt offended that their human took on another: their territory was invaded. Even the more relaxed cats needed their own space sometimes. It was only cat to want to have some alone time. Those two were the exception. There was no way that one would be found without the other. They'd probably die together. They couldn't live without each other. I soon grew bored of them.

My eyes settled on the red cat sat at the back. I'd never seen that cat before. Its fur was stained a red-almost-orange colour. It didn't look natural. It was almost as though it'd been painted. The fur was bright white underneath. They were large with blue eyes. I saw I was making them nervous; they were trying to avoid eye contact. As I continued to stare, I took in the large frame and the strange jaw that almost hung loose at the lips. I knew that cat. Of course, I did! The cat was One Fang!

The sneaky mutt had turned up in disguise, and scared my tail! He was no more scared than a cat about to make a terrific hunt. Of course he was there. He had to see the result of the day for himself. There was no way that he could stay away. Wouldn't want the other cats to have to fill him in because they might leave out important details. Didn't he trust his whisperer or watcher? Obviously not. Cats who had other decent cats on their side knew to trust them, their every word, their every intonation when speaking, and their intentions. I had no idea who One Fang's whisperer or watcher was, but I revelled in the knowledge that he didn't trust them.

Usually, cats who were untrusting of their team of cats had good reason to be cautious. However, they were usually misguided in their mistrust of others. Decent cats knew that the only cat they couldn't trust to do the job right was themselves. That was how they became insecure. Somewhere in their lives, they'd betrayed another and were punished heavily for it. Strangely, they never seemed to learn their insecurities stemmed from themselves. Instead, they illogically and irrationally placed their mistrust onto other cats. Their relationships forever broke down with watchers and whisperers. If questioned about how it broke down, they always gave the same excuse and couldn't trust their team cats. Usually, there was a better reason. They usually spent so much time cross-referencing tuna from their watchers, whisperers or both, they didn't keep their eye on the prize. Cats don't like not to be untrusted, especially by their own cats. Whisperers and watchers have a complex network of informants. They always find out when a cat is combing through their work.

I had to play this one right. I had to source who One Fang's watcher and whisperers were. I knew that there was no way that Brown Crown was fulfilling either of those roles; he was too publicly known, especially after the trial. I knew that neither Curly nor Stripes worked for him. That ruled out five cats, including him. I saw that ten cats filled a row, so that meant two rows of five. There were five rows, so fifty cats in total. It couldn't be any of the cats on his own row that'd be stupid. Nine and five made fourteen, so that narrowed it down to thirty-six.

One Fang had clearly snuck in, as one of the last cats and didn't want to be seen. I assumed that he didn't even want his team knowing that he was there, so that ruled out the row in front.

There was no way that the Skittle Twins were any of these. They were caught by surprise when I walked onto their land. That made twenty-four possibilities.

Old Ginger Paws could not be a part of his intricate team for two reasons. He wasn't inconspicuous enough with his red fur, and these cats had to be fit enough to climb high or slender enough to keep low and dash and squeeze through small spaces. This tuna alone allowed me to drop another eight cats. There were fifteen cats left, and six were kittens. Only a fool would choose a kitten to be a full-time whisperer or watcher. They weren't fully trained or grown and tired easily. That ruled out some of the older cats too, with the circle of life. That left four possibilities: a patched cat against white, an all-white cat, a tabby cat, and a black cat. That was easy. It was the last two. They could be inconspicuous.

The tabby and the black cat of course sat in different places. The black cat was on the front row; the tabby was on the third row. The tabby started to make conversation with his neighbour. It was clear that the tabby wanted to remain a part of the crowd. It was easier for a black cat. They were able to stay incognito. Immediately, I knew that the black cat had to be the whisperer because they have to hide in the shadows.

I locked eyes with the whisperer, enough to make her feel uncomfortable and to send a message. I made the black cat stare back at me, so that I could direct the whisperer to lift her gaze with only my eyes. The black cat turned her head and looked at the, sprayed-red cat on the back row. Her tail bushed out, probably from anger that I'd figured out whose team she was on. Or perhaps she was angry because One Fang didn't trust her. I suspected it was the latter.

One Fang was sat too far back to be able to see what I was doing. To him, it looked as though I only sat there staring at the gallery. Whatever the outcome of the bench was, I felt good knowing that I'd created a stir. The black cat wouldn't be working for One Fang long, not now that she knew that One Fang didn't trust her to do her job. I needed to protect Skinny's land and ensure One Fang didn't get the land, even if I was subject to a locked-in order forever. If Skinny Hind was gone forever, I felt good knowing that the land would never be One Fang's. That was my parting gift to Skinny Hind, dead or alive. One Fang longed to take territory on Skinny's land, bitter knowing that it'd never be his. That was justice enough for me.

# 6

## VICTORY?

I wasn't sure how long the bench deliberated over the verdict because it felt like forever that I sat alone on the stand. I was relieved when I saw their faces come back into the room. I had to hand it to them. They were stoic, regardless of their decision. I had no idea whether or not that was a good thing. Some cats liked being able to exert power over others, which was unhealthy. They usually went straight to a locked-in order. Other cats tried their hardest to ensure the cat maintained their freedom and were solemn with their lack of a choice. I was in such a nervous state; I couldn't rely on my instinct.

They remained silent as they each took their seats at the bench. My angst only grew.

"Inspector White Tip, we apologise for the time taken to make our decision. As I'm sure you will appreciate, decisions for charges of treason take some consideration," the Bengal explained.

At that point, the mention of treason, made me think that my chances were up. I was about to become incarcerated in my human's home. Of course I liked my permanent home, but a place could become a prison pretty quickly when there was nowhere to escape to. I still nodded to show my respect.

"Having said that, if a cat relinquishes their land for a period of time, that means that it was, in fact, your land and remained so whilst you used it as a point of entry to inspect Skinny Hind's land. We believe that there was no real threat to the Skittle Twins; therefore, no treason could've been committed. You didn't act in a threatening matter, simply by approaching them to ask for access to perform an investigation," the Bengal said.

"As for the charge of unreasonable force, there isn't enough evidence to suggest who made the first move. However, it's clear to the Council that this was a simple cat fight and not a matter for the Council to decide on. Mr Crown, please advise Mr Fang that he works on his confidence to walk freely in the Neighbourhood, as should be any cat's right. We don't believe that either cat has acted unreasonably."

"What remains unclear is whether or not Skinny Hind is alive. Therefore, we're granting you, Inspector White Tip, four days to report back to the bench on the confirmation of Mr Hind's disappearance. If Mr Hind hasn't returned, and you're still unsure of whether or not he lives, his land will be auctioned off to any wanting cats," the Bengal continued.

"Thank you. I appreciate you granting me four days," I said.

I had no idea which cats believed my story. It didn't actually matter to me; I was just grateful that there weren't any restraints on my freedom. If I was totally honest, I'm not sure that I could've lived with that. I'd have broken it soon enough and landed myself back into trouble again.

"Inspector White Tip, I imagine that you have a lot to get back to," the Bengal said. "Any other cat found on the land of Skinny Hind will be summoned at once. The land is out of bounds for four days to enable Inspector White Tip to investigate without tampering of evidence."

The room suddenly grew louder as the cats in the gallery left. I kept my eye on the black cat. She was about to make a decent move. She swiftly exited the room, tracing One Fang without making it obvious. I had a feeling that she was going to resign from her post with One Fang pretty quickly. I turned to Stripes, but she was gone. I assumed that she'd headed back to her post.

I wondered whether watchers ever worked together. It made sense that they would, just like the whisperers. There were things that they might miss given their location and position, but it soon occurred that they always seemed like solitary cats. I never really saw them with any other cats. Maybe that was because cats only look up to the skies when they're tracing birds or insects. Their desire isn't to see anything at ground-level, but even the watchers looked down most of the time. Maybe that was something that needed to change. Maybe I needed to expand my network.

Then again, it did seem like a lot of effort. Trusting two cats was easier to manage. I didn't need the hassle of a large network of cats who split off into their own little sectors. Besides, I didn't want Stripes to feel like her nose was being pushed out for another. She was the best watcher that I knew, and she had the best spot. I wasn't about to jeopardise that for anything.

My chest swelled with pride as I left The Burrow. I knew straight away where I was heading to celebrate. I looked across at Curly Whiskers. His eyes started to sparkle. This was the best outcome.

The crowd swept me along, and I soon found myself alone. As I headed along the path that led me back to the Neighbourhood, I realised that I suddenly felt quite lost. I hadn't paid much attention to where we were walking. Jet and Ebony just seemed to lead me there and because I was so consumed with dread, I hardly paid attention to the direction in which we were heading. The night began to descend upon the skies, casting shadows all around. There was a chill that seemed to electrocute my fur. I wasn't sure of myself.

Doubt and fear filled me. I realised that One Fang had to know his way to the Council, or, at least other cats who knew the way. How else would they have known that I was on the Skittle Twins' land? They were never going to tell anyone that I was there. How had they made their way here? Those two cats were afraid of their own fur and rarely ventured beyond their human's land. They must have been chaperoned. How did they attend the Council's meetings when they could barely face the Neighbourhood? None of it made sense to me.

Without notice, I felt my heart pounding against my chest. Nighttime was supposed to be the best time for a cat to use his or her instincts, yet my instincts headed overboard. Every slight rustle of leaves in the wind left me feeling scared to my wits. Everything about me wanted to be back in the Neighbourhood where I could feel safe. Who knew what animals could be found there? When the whole path was shrouded in darkness, I ran until I saw light again.

I scrambled up the fence with all of my might. I felt twigs scratching at my legs and face. I knew that I was bleeding when I felt something warm trickle down my face. I stood on the top and wasn't sure what I was jumping down onto, but I took the leap of faith that I was going to feel safer on the other side.

The pain of One Fang's bite was nothing compared to the pain of the landing. I felt something sharp pierce through my rear left paw. Whatever it was, hurt even more when I pulled my paw back; it tore the claw. I continued to walk forward, limping on my foot as the pain seared through my foot until I couldn't bear weight on it any longer.

As I stumbled towards the gate, my paw throbbed with every step. I felt weak and defenceless, so when I heard the snarling I almost gave up.

I could barely see the beast behind the teeth that gleamed in the moonlight. It gnashed its teeth at me furiously. I knew that if I walked slowly, the beast would follow my treads at a pace. However, if I ran, the beast would most definitely outrun me, especially when I was injured. I walked slowly, taking deep breaths to buy me enough time to get to the gate. I leapt up, catching the fence just right.

The beast growled and jumped frantically at the fence. The fence shook with such ferocity that I nearly fell back to the ground into its jaws. I flung myself onto the other side in the vain hope that I was finally meeting safety.

When I saw the four sets of green eyes on me, I knew that I'd entered some new nightmare. My paw felt like it was practically hanging off. I didn't have the strength or inclination to have a fight. There was no way that I was going to win with four on one.

I stood transfixed. I waited for them to crawl out from under the car, one by one. I needed to buy myself a minute to make a plan.

# 7

## QUICK THINKING SKILLS

All cats have to be quick thinkers, whether or not they live with humans makes no difference, even for those who throw away their freedom. For the latter, it can be worse; they never know when things might change. This happened to my friend Sphinx.

Sphinx was, as the name suggests, a hairless, pedigree Sphinx cat. Some humans loved their cats bald; others found them repulsive. To those that love them, they are an expensive and delicate breed.

Sphinx began life with a human who was Heiress to a fortune. She was in her seventies when she picked him up as a kitten. She made reassurances for if she ever died, and he survived her.

When the Heiress passed away, Sphinx then went to live with one of the Heiress' cousins. He had a comfortable life with the cousin. Sometimes she forgot that she'd fed him and fed him two or three extra meals a day, but then other days she forgot altogether. The cousin never gave any reassurance for what should happen to Sphinx if he survived her.

The cousin became ill. Sphinx claimed that when it went from two of them to sometimes having five or six people around, the cousin grew confused and then had to leave her home. When she did, they tried to put Sphinx into a metal crate. He worried and hissed, spat and scratched the warden, then made his escape.

Escapes can sound exciting, but they're not. Without a plan or the skills to survive, Sphinx had no idea how to hunt for himself. He'd never developed that skill. He had no idea how to cross a road, bathe himself, or fight. For him starting from fresh was worse. These are things cats need to learn from their mother, and judging by their breed, she probably didn't know these things either. He had to learn to think quickly and fast.

Sphinx happened to find himself in our neighbourhood purely by accident. He walked and walked until he could barely walk anymore.

Curly, feeling sorry for him, spent a long time teaching Sphinx how to hunt because there was no way that he was ever going to fight. He didn't have it in him, which meant that there were only specific times when he could and would venture out to find food. There is a quiet time for cats, but only for a few minutes.

Roaming cats hunt in the night and have the strongest instincts. They tend to be the best fighters too. The two strengths seemed to go hand in hand. They rested during the day under a car, tree, or bush. Human-tamed cats tend to go out as the sun is rising, ready to catch the early bird as a morning snack, then they go inside and rest in the mid-morning. It was the perfect time for Sphinx to go hunting. He had a better chance of catching something.

My humans' house is on the road. It isn't that busy, but I still have to know about cars and crossing the road. I've watched friends and foes get hit by cars. If they do survive, they tend to live a tough existence. My pal, Smoky, was hit by a car. He still gets around, but he gets tired without his extra leg. He's still a good fighter though, the old rascal. But knowing how to cross the road and move fast wasn't going to be enough for this dilemma.

I'll be honest, when I need to be, or it's a choice, I'm a good fighter. I look big and some of the kitty-cats think that I'll be sluggish. What they don't know is that I make sure I can climb a fence every day. I make sure I practice when no one is around to see, except humans, and who are they going to tell? I run a mile every day. I also sharpen my claws for fun each morning, noon, and night. The kitty-cats assume because they're lean and quick that I can't fight as well. But I can. It's all an illusion and I stand my ground. I only use half of my strength for those that come close. The only need a fair warning. If they get persistent, I add a bit more to my swipe. As for the truly obnoxious ones who think they have an entitlement to land because they say so, well, I make sure I give full strength with non-retracted claws. I also give more than one swipe as well whilst they're down. I make sure that they know I don't give my land up to anyone. I don't need to shout about it; it's not a challenge. I just defend what I've earned.

I realised that I had to use my fighting strength to help me; alongside my inspector skills and my hunting skills. For example, a flock of birds is almost impossible to hunt – the flock becomes the distraction. Most cats walk away. To hunt from a flock, a cat has to single out a weak one. It's not easy, but it's usually one that flies within the bottom quarter and never reaches the top quarter. Their flight is shorter and less elegant. Then, the weakest is easier to track. The flock swirls to protect the weak by flying in front. However, if a cat swipes as though they were going to clean themselves, they can have the bird in a second. There are so many distractions for the birds to contend with while keeping themselves moving, they don't realise the one that's gone.

The four cats were meeting me like a pack. The front was a guard, the strongest, and the shield of the pack, but not necessarily the best. The two on either side were the swords. The back was the weakest and gave the last swipe, if they needed to. I had to break them up, so I created a circle around them by walking around the perimeter of their gang. It meant that each cat had to turn to look at me and then move to defend the weakest one. As I did this, I chiselled away at the surface, by sneakily swiping at the swords, which meant that the shield had to move faster. Though the shield was the strength, he wasn't necessarily the fittest. As the swords were being hit, they had little defence, and as they were kitty-cats, and I soon won the fight.

I walked with my head held high, but inside I prayed for a miracle. I couldn't handle anything else. I was in pain and exhausted. I wanted to be with the Duchess and my other humans, fast.

I'd lived more than one night on the streets. I knew I could survive that. I'd spent months at a time on the streets before I was taken in by the Duchess and the other humans, but I was younger and had quicker reactions. A cat's instincts become second-nature when they're used enough. I needed my humans badly. I was bleeding and I knew that one more thing might've kept me away from finding out what happened to Skinny, and I only had four days.

If I didn't rest, I knew that I'd suffer total burn out.

# 8

## MERLIN

I found myself in a delirious state from the pain. My body disobeyed orders from my mind. I kept myself to the road so that no cats could accuse me of trespassing on their land. I knew that I couldn't handle another fight. I resigned myself to the knowledge that if I was set upon by another cat, I'd lose at the very least. I stopped looking down at my paw because all I saw was a bloody mess entangled in my fur. It made me feel worse when I looked at it.

Though I had no idea where I was headed. All I can remember was that I kept telling myself that I had to keep moving. The last thing that I wanted was hyperthermia. It was the middle of Autumn and the air felt cool when the sun went down. My fur was no longer doing its usual good job. I was fully aware of the fact that I needed to get home and fast.

Between Stripes and Curly Whiskers, I was never going to be lost for long. They had the run of the streets and they knew the Neighbourhood well enough to know when I was veering towards the border and then edging into another neighbourhood. Stripes later confided in me, that she watched the same spot for so long whilst waiting for my return, she climbed down from her viewing point to seek out Curly.

Of course, Curly knew she'd be on her way when he hadn't seen me either. He'd started to gather tuna from other cats around the Neighbourhood to find me.

When they came to my rescue, they said that I was in the worse state they'd ever seen me. All I saw was two shadows walking towards me. I had no idea who they belonged to. I remember feeling an urge to want to protect myself. Neither looked particularly threatening, but I was confused. I started to hiss and spit at them to warn them off coming near me.

I've no idea how they managed to persuade me that they weren't a threat; I think the pain begged for it be over. At that point, I would've accepted help from One Fang if it'd come to it. Thankfully, it didn't.

Somehow, they got me to the Duchess and the Male One, but I was in a sorry state. My fur was matted to my paw. I'd walked a long distance, which caused dirt to enter the wound. I've never willingly stepped into the crate to take me to the vet, but I didn't put up a fight either. At that point, I knew I needed help. Sometimes a cat just knows.

The worst thing about seeing the vet is sharing the waiting room with the dogs. The dogs can never just sit and wait to be seen; they have to show that their sense of smell is working and sniff us out straight away. Then, they feel the need to alert the whole waiting room to us cats being there. They never respect cats' right to privacy. As if that wasn't bad enough, when we got upset, dogs got territorial, as though it was their vet first before we came along. Well, they can have the vets. No cat wants them.

As soon as I stepped onto the metal table, I knew that my vet was a dog lover. Even before I saw the dog paraphernalia with the clock around the Labrador's face and the calendar with a litter of Dachshunds on, the vet had an overly keen smile on her face as though we were going to be friends. We weren't. Her hair was the curly kind that looked like it belonged on a poodle. It didn't help that she had tied it into two round pompoms on the side of her head. She lifted the lid of my crate when I laid down, and she caught my paw as she reached in to lift me out. Even if it was by accident, she really should've known better.

"He has a poorly paw that has become a little infected," she said. A dog could've diagnosed that.

When she wanted to examine the rest of me, I didn't trust her because she was definitely a dog person. I bit her, so she knew that I wasn't about to agree to an examination. I had my diagnosis and prescription. I had work to do and I wanted to be out of there as soon as possible.

"I think Oscar must be in a little bit of pain. I don't want to aggravate him anymore, so I'll just give him his antibiotics and then he can be on his way," she said.

Oscar is my human-cat name. All cats have a human-cat name when they live with humans. They have their real name, which usually comes from a trait of the cat, like their looks, character or personality. White Tip came from my tail. I was pleased to have a good name. It was far better than Dock, who had her tail docked as a kitten. As if the memory wasn't painful enough, she had a daily reminder whenever someone said her name. She always claimed that she didn't mind and thought it showed she was a survivor, but I always thought it was an awful name. I refused to call her by her street name, so I called her by her human-cat name, Doris. She said she didn't mind whatever cats called her, but I used to see her smile after saying her name.

If cats in the Neighbourhood called me Oscar, I ignored them. They knew my street name, and only humans call their cats by the name they gave them. I divulge for a reason because what happened next was a pivotal point in the case.

Skinny Hind's human obviously never called him Skinny Hind. Instead, his name was Merlin. As the humans discussed my treatment, I settled down into my crate to show that I wanted to go home.

When we stepped outside, the human behind the desk picked up my medicine and then said,

"There seem to be a lot of things happening on Crescent Drive this week. Is he a friend of Merlin's?"

There was only one cat called Merlin on Crescent Drive, and that was Skinny Hind! I knew from the tone of her voice that he had to be alive. She wouldn't have sounded so chirpy if he'd died. She would've been far more morose.

"I'm not sure, Oscar likes to keep his friends and family separate," the Male One said.

I wasn't so sure what the joke was, but the lady and the Male One seemed to find it funny. Humans could be simple, funny creatures at times. I just wanted the Male One to take me home immediately. I had things to sort out and tuna to pass on. I was glad that the strange jokes stopped at one. My eyes were hurting from rolling.

"It says here that Oscar will need to stay inside for two days," the strange lady said.

Two days! There was no way that I was going to be staying indoors for two days. No. I was working on borrowed time. I had to make sure that I had something to tell the Cat Council. There was no way that they were going to grant me an extension, especially not if I wasn't there to ask for one.

My mind started to race back and forth as I tried to think of solutions. There were many, but few were plausible or even possible. I needed both of my humans to be distracted and there was little chance of that. The Male One was easier to distract than the Duchess. Added to that, I needed them both to be distracted whilst the door to the outside was open. I had to be swift enough to actually escape, whilst not drawing attention to myself. That was going to be a challenge.

# 9

# DRUMMING MY CLAWS

I was miserable for the whole journey. I hated car journeys even at the best of times. It wasn't easy to stay steady. I don't like to be forced to lie down, but I had no choice in the crate. There was no room to sit down or stand up. The floor was always slippery. As soon as the car started moving, my balance was whipped away. Next, I couldn't see anything but the edge of the window and the door, so the view was boring. Then, I had the added misery of knowing that time wasn't on my side. I hated knowing that I had to accept defeat. None of the circumstances were working in my favour. I was fresh out of luck.

"There's no way that we can keep him inside for two days," the Duchess said.

My ears pricked up. I loved the Duchess. She always came through for me with her reasoning.

"I think we should follow the vet's advice," the Male One said.

I had to put both paws over my mouth to stop myself from hissing at him. I didn't want him to know that I was listening. If he knew that I could hear the conversation and understand it, he'd expect me to become a performer and know I did what I wanted to. That was a bad move; humans should never know a cat's level of understanding.

52

"Oscar is a wild animal. He literally needs his freedom to roam. If he loses territory, he is going to have to fight again," the Duchess said. "You know that I'm right."

It was spooky how much she did know. That was exactly it. I hated having to return to the Neighbourhood when I'd been on holiday because it always meant shooing turf trespassers off my land. It was a bother that I could do without. I wasn't really comfortable with the humans knowing that of course, but she was right.

"I know," the Male One said. "I just don't want him to get hurt."

"I know, but maybe if we keep him in for one night, then we can let him outside," the Duchess suggested.

One day wasn't so bad, but it wasn't ideal. The ideal thing would've been to have all four days to investigate, but I had to accept that was never going to happen. The Duchess was never going to let me go outside on day one.

"Let's see how he is first, and then maybe he can go outside if he's better than he has been," the Male One said.

That seemed like a good solution. I knew what I had to do. I had the day to rest and sleep, which I welcomed wholeheartedly. I'd barely slept since Stripes and Curly Whiskers found me. I needed some time to rest and recuperate. Sleep sounded like a dream. Then, once I'd rested, I knew I could show my best side, and the Duchess was bound to let me out of the house, even if the Male One didn't agree.

As soon as we arrived back home, Stripes and Curly were sat on the driveway, awaiting my arrival. I'm not going to lie; I loved the homecoming attention. It also meant that I was able to pass on the tuna to them. All was good.

"Look at that! Those cheeky cats are on our drive!" the Male One shouted. "I'm not carrying him out whilst they're there. I'll let you in, and then I need you to bring the hose around."

I tried my utmost to show that I liked the cats, but the journey shook me up. My fur stood on end, and my tail was bushy. There was no chance that I was able to persuade my humans that Curly and Stripes were friends. The humans were going to chase them off my land.

The Duchess left the car before I even had a chance to open my mouth. I scratched at the door of the crate frantically.

"It's okay Oscar. They'll be gone before you get out," the Male One said.

I literally scuppered myself. I should've stayed calm and kept still, then my fur would've settled, and the hose wouldn't have touched Stripes and Curly. They were going to be furious. A little bit of me laughed inside because it was about time Curly was gotten back by something. It was nearly always me that he swiped. It was his signature move.

The Male One turned the hose on them. Stripes scarpered pretty quickly. I think the only part of her that was soaked was her tail. Curly sat stoically, waiting. He looked like a drowned rat.

"This one is so cheeky. He's staying despite me using the hose to chase him off," the Male One said. "Do you think I should just carry him into the house? He doesn't seem to be bothered by it."

"Yeah just bring him in," the Duchess said.

As the Male One carried me back into the house, I took my chance to tell Curly about Skinny Hind.

"Curly I think Skinny Hind might be alive," I said.

"How do you know?" Curly asked.

"The vets mentioned that I was the second cat from Crescent Drive. He has to be alive," I said.

There was no time to explain anymore. I just knew that I had to leave Curly with that nugget of tuna, and he'd have to link the dots together. I knew that would normally have been my job, but I also knew that I had to get bed rest – vet's orders.

As soon as the door opened, I stepped out into my palace, stretching my legs and sinking my claws into the carpet. I hated many things that about the vets – the smell of disinfectant, the amount of hairs from a range of cats, and even worse dogs. I always felt like I needed a bath after going there, and I *hate* baths. I gave myself a quick wash and cleared my schedule. I lay down on my bed. I had at least twenty-four hours to catch up on. I looked forward to every single one.

# 10

## MAGPIE IN PAW

I t was almost a shame when the two days of sleep were over. I knew that the first stop I had to make was with my watcher, Stripes. I looked out to make sure that no cats were going to stop me along the way to refight to defend my land. Time was precious. I didn't need anything slowing me down.

There was a nice pair of magpies hopping on the front lawn of my access house. I pounced just in time. I knew I had no time to fight, but I also knew that I had to give Stripes a peace offering after the Male One soaked her. I quickly chowed down on mine before carrying hers over.

I waited at the first-floor roof for Stripes, as I usually did. It had been nearly a week. I'm not going to lie; it was tough even mustering the strength to jump to this level. I called her down.

Stripes landed within seconds. She grabbed the magpie and looked to leave immediately.

"I'm sorry, I tried my best, but my humans are very protective," I said.

"We were there to welcome you home," Stripes spat.

"I know you were, but my paws were tied. I'll make sure that I bring a catch every day for a week," I said.

"Two weeks, and you need to get One Fang off his land and quickly," she said.

That was enough to make me livid. One Fang knew that he had to stay away from Skinny Hind's land for at least four days. I still had twenty-four hours. He had no right and he knew that. What was he doing? "Two weeks it is," I said.

Stripes headed back up to her watch spot whilst I headed over to Skinny's land. I wanted to spot One Fang going against the Council. That cat needed to be removed from the Neighbourhood once and for all.

I should've known that Curly Whiskers always managed to find me before I found him. I felt the scratch and then heard him laughing, his signature move. I knew that he hadn't taken the soaking badly. I crawled underneath the car to where Curly was hiding out.

"I know Stripes has told you that One Fang has the land occupied. He's been in there since you went to the other neighbourhood," Curly said.

"How did he know that I'd gone missing? He no longer has a whisperer," I said.

I thought back to three days ago when I was on the stand for the Council. The black cat was definitely his whisperer. She was offended that he'd betrayed her by showing up at the trial and not trusting her. How was it that she'd forgiven him? Maybe it was stupidity; maybe she was biding her time. Either way, there was no way that she was passing on tuna to him. She was too frustrated for that.

"One Fang has multiple whisperers. He always has," Curly explained.

"I don't understand. He was at my trial. He painted himself and sat at the back, watching the whole thing. I found his whisperer. She was a black cat. When I locked eyes with her, I directed her eyes to where he was sitting. She was furious," I explained.

"We don't know whether that was all part of the plan. Shadows still works for him. He might've betrayed her, but she's still in the inner circle," Curly said.

"Why would she still be working for him when he betrayed her like that?" I asked.

"Who knows?" he shrugged. "I imagine that he has promised her something and that she's biding her time. It's no use trying to get revenge on a cat like One Fang. His operation is far too large."

"Not to mention that he is persistent," I added.

I felt bitter that not even the Cat Council was enough of a threat to ward him off. I felt defeated knowing that he'd gone onto Skinny's land regardless of the consequences. It was so disrespectful and bullish to expect that he could just do whatever he wanted. If all cats did that, then the Neighbourhood would be in a state of lawlessness. There'd be no cohesion —every cat for himself. We'd be forever fighting. I also hated knowing that I had to compromise my beliefs. Skinny was going to return home, and he'd have to fight for the occupation of his human's home. That wasn't fair. Every cat had right to the occupation of their own human's home.

I wanted nothing more than to seek my revenge on One Fang, but Curly was right – his operation was too large. I needed something bigger and better.

"Don't do it, White Tip. You know that this will only end in trouble," Curly warned.

"Do we just leave this war for Skinny to fight?" I asked.

Curly looked back at me. It wasn't often that he took time to think. He was always one step ahead, so to see him deliberate over any form of a decision was somewhat disconcerting.

"I don't know if we can raise the numbers that we'd need to in order to overthrow him, but Skinny can't do it alone," Curly said. "We haven't got long."

"How many are we talking?" I asked.

In my mind, I wanted to double whatever his number was. Sheer numbers were the only way to overthrow him. It was going to be a challenge to raise the numbers without his knowledge.

"I don't know. Maybe ten," Curly replied.

It wasn't impossible. There were plenty of cats who attended the trial. The problem was I had no idea who they were. I wasn't a cat who wanted to expand into the Neighbourhood. I preferred to stay inconspicuous. I liked to keep my numbers low to make sure I could trust and form a bond with them. Any form of betrayal meant something so huge that most cats just didn't have the gall. Clearly, One Fang wasn't one of those cats. He ruled in numbers.

"We need someone on the Council," I said.

I considered which members I might be able to persuade. The Bengal was too elite for us to find out where she reigned. The British Short Hair wasn't my kind of cat. He seemed too similar to One Fang in the way he sought his answers. Jet, Ebony and the Ragdoll were much better choices. They all appeared much more objective.

Curly wasn't keen on the British Short Hair either. He watched his reactions at the trial and didn't trust him. He seemed furious when the Bengal dropped the treason charge. He glared at her when she awarded me time to investigate Skinny's land. Curly believed that he'd have quite easily have issued a locked-in order if he had the chance to. I thought so too.

Curly was also reluctant to involve Jet and Ebony because they never asked any questions at the trial. He had a point. They probably didn't have much power, if they never spoke. Were they afraid? Bored? I wasn't so keen on Jet because she always struck me as a lazy cat. She wasn't alert enough to know what was going on in the Neighbourhood. She spent the majority of her time sleeping. I assumed that she only woke to eat.

My gut instinct went with the Ragdoll. She was fair, much more empathetic, had good instincts and acted with her emotions. I knew in my gut that she'd be furious that One Fang had gone against their decision.

"The Ragdoll?" Curly said, before I even managed to open my mouth.

Curly was exactly the reason why I chose to operate with only two. He knew my thoughts before I needed to express them. He read me well and was able to act on the tuna easily.

I looked up at Stripes. She already signalled with her head where to find the Ragdoll. I bowed my head in appreciation.

"I need to get to her, without anyone knowing. Better yet, I need her to get to me. What's the Ragdoll like with heights?" I asked.

"There's only one way to find out. We need to ask her," Curly said.

"I also want Brown Crown," I said.

I needed someone who could lie through their teeth, but even better, I needed a cat who others believed. I knew that there was no way that I'd be able to trust him. He was fickle. I had to offer him something that he really needed, something that One Fang couldn't. He was smart enough to get One Fang away from the trial. I needed his brains.

"You need Squirrel," Curly said.

"Who's Squirrel?" I asked.

"You'll see, and you'll know why when you meet him," Curly said. "Then you're not going to like these suggestions, but the Skittle Twins are more valuable than you give them credit for."

My fur stood on end. How was I able to trust the Skittle Twins after what they had done? They were fickle and scared of everything. They nearly cost me my freedom. I was ready to hiss at him. What a suggestion!

"I'm just thinking that we need members of the Council to agree to have him placed under a locked-in order. That is the only way that we are going to defeat him. We need to disarm him by sending him inside. If we go directly to the Council now without supporters, we might not get the order granted. If we have supporters, the more we have, the more likely it is that the order will be granted." Curly said.

The most infuriating thing was that Curly was right. A locked-in order was the only way to disarm One Fang. There was no way that any of his gang were going to turn on him; they were too frightened. I was going to have to go be the bigger cat and go with my food bowl in hand.

*Full Moon*

# 11

## GAINING ALLIES

The first cat I went to see was the Ragdoll. I couldn't bring myself to speak to the Skittle Twins; I had to work myself up to them. I knew from their fickle nature that they'd agree to work with me immediately, and then the minute that One Fang or any of his followers came along, they'd switch to the other side. I'd already had my paws burned once, I wasn't about to have them burned again. I needed followers who I could rely on.

Curly checked with his network whether the Ragdoll would meet me above ground. She refused. I had to approach her, on her land and I headed over straight away.

There was an immediate change of air as I started to ascend towards the Ragdoll's property. It was only a slight incline, but the houses were immediately larger and fancier right away. I should've known: she was a pedigree cat. I knew I'd arrived when I saw the stone plaques with her face chiselled into them. They were fancy.

My only issue was that I had no idea how I would approach the Ragdoll or when she was going to appear. All I knew from humans of pedigrees were they were usually very fussy about when their cats could explore the Neighbourhood. Some were only allowed to sit in the windows of their houses watching the world go by, and some had curfews. I knew that the Ragdoll at least ventured outside. My problem was that she was likely to have a schedule, and time was slipping through my paws.

I sat waiting. The last thing that I wanted was to alarm the Ragdoll. I wanted her to be on my side because she felt the need to uphold loyalty, rather than because she feared me. I didn't want to alarm her. I tidied myself up a bit, then a black cat with a white face crawled out from under a car and approached me.

"Inspector White Tip?" he said.

"That's right. Are you Full Moon?" I asked.

Full Moon nodded his head. Curly Whiskers said that he'd spread the word amongst his best whisper comrades. He hoped that Full Moon would be there first because he trusted him the most. It was my first time meeting Full Moon, I kept myself to my land mostly, and this was a little outside of my boundaries. He seemed like a decent cat. He was a little unusual because his fur seemed fairly long.

"The Ragdoll will be waiting in her garden house," Full Moon said and signalled with his head that I needed to follow.

As we walked through the iron gates towards the back of the house, I noticed that his tail was furless and the tip of it was missing. It made me wince. I'd no idea how it'd happened. Curly never shared this tuna with me, but that was serious. Cats didn't just lose the tips of their tails. He also walked with a subtle limp – that made two of us. My paw had stopped bleeding, but the cut hadn't healed.

I was curious to know how Full Moon had such a strong link with the Ragdoll. It seemed so unlikely that they'd work together. He seemed like a common cat, and she was a pedigree. It was good that she didn't look down her nose at us. I imagined that some of the Council didn't like to mix with the cats lower down in the Neighbourhood. They thought we were beneath them.

The garden house was something I'd never seen before. I needed one of those. First, it had two stories. I walked up the ramp to the top floor, where she sat waiting. My paws felt like they were in heaven. I'd never felt underground heating before; it felt wonderful.

"Inspector White Tip, please take a seat," the Ragdoll said.

It was one of those situations where I needed to wait to speak. An invitation to sit down wasn't an invitation to talk. Besides, I was curious to know why the Ragdoll agreed to speak to me. It had to mean that she had her suspicions herself. Members of the Council were usually unreachable unless they wanted to speak to a common street cat.

"I hear that you have news for me about Skinny Hind," the Ragdoll said. "Off you go, Full Moon."

Full Moon appeared unaffected. He left stoically. It was obvious that she wore the studded collar. The cats listened to her. In my eyes, that was a positive. If she spoke to all of her followers that way, and they took it without offence, that meant that there had to be more of them. I felt hopeful. Full Moon sat outside the garden house, keeping guard. I'd never felt more protected.

"I've news that Skinny Hind might be alive," I said.

"Inspector White Tip, you have less than twenty-four hours. We need to have a little more than a *might*. We need a guarantee," the Ragdoll warned.

"It doesn't mean anything if he is alive," I said bitterly.

"What do you mean Inspector?" the Ragdoll asked.

"You gave me a free pass for four days, yet One Fang has the land occupied. Who's looking out for Skinny Hind? The Council certainly aren't," I said.

"You're wrong," the Ragdoll said.

"Take a look for yourself," I said.

The Ragdoll called Full Moon back into the garden house. For a cat with a limp, Full Moon sure was swift. I thought Curly was quick off the mark, but he had nothing on Full Moon, who was fast.

"I need you to check out Skinny Hind's land, and I need to know who has it occupied. You need to do this undetected. One Fang might be the culprit. Send Autumn," the Ragdoll ordered.

Who knew how long it'd take? I felt apprehensive, even though I trusted Curly. There was no reason for him to betray me. I needed one of One Fang's cats to be there to make sure that what I was saying could be corroborated. I usually checked the tuna out for myself when it involved bringing in the power cats, but this was time-sensitive. I hoped that whoever Autumn was, that he or she was as swift as Full Moon.

Just as my nerves were starting to ease, Patches burst through the door. The Ragdoll sat up. He wasn't expecting to see anyone besides the Ragdoll. Patches hissed with his back arched towards the Ragdoll. I knew that a cat like the Ragdoll wasn't used to fighting, especially when caught off-guard. She was a pedigree cat and deserved to be treated and respected. Her eyes were wide, like saucers. It was unfair. He knew that she'd be defenceless. I was surprised too, when she didn't run.

I hissed. I wanted Patches to turn around. Just because he had no morals, and took cats by surprise, that didn't mean that I needed to act like that. I still had my integrity, plus I wanted to see the look of surprise on his face when he saw me.

I'd seen Patches around the Neighbourhood. He was an alley cat, without an alley. I had no idea where his land was – if he had any – but he was wily. I needed to know whether he was as good a fighter, as he was cunning.

Patches spun around. His fur appeared electrified. I lashed out quickly, before he had a chance to attack me. When his head rose, the blood only made him look more menacing. The scratches on his head made him look tougher, but I remained strong. I lashed out again. A smart cat would've known to move. I struck him in the same place. It had to hurt, or he was much tougher than I realised. He swayed a little, but not much. Fear and anger pulsed through my veins.

Full Moon burst into the garden house before either of us had the chance to fight anymore. He sank his claws into Patches and removed him from the garden house in one fell swoop. I was seriously impressed. I no longer cared about the Ragdoll, I wanted Full Moon on my side.

Patches sprinted off the land. I knew where he was headed. We had less time than I thought. Soon, all of One Fang's gang would've informed him that he was being watched.

"We need to move – now!" I shouted.

Sahara

Dolly

# 12

## ROOM WITH A VIEW

As we walked to the Stables, I realised that I'd explored very little of the Neighbourhood. I stuck to my land but needed to venture out more. I'd barely seen anything and only had four houses. The field looked vast. I'd seen it there, but I'd avoided it in case of foxes. There was little that I was afraid of, but I wasn't going to extend that courage to foxes.

Foxes were like dogs. Their teeth were sharp. They could tear us apart in minutes. Foxes belonged in the wild; humans never tamed them. They relied on their instincts to get by.

"Aren't there foxes here?" I blurted out.

The Ragdoll looked at me, disgusted. Full Moon walked on, silently. It wasn't a stupid question. I'd never treaded on that path before. How was I to know?

"If we do see one, we'll have Lock Jaw," Full Moon said, finally.

"No, he's too unpredictable," the Ragdoll said.

"One Fang can be managed," Full Moon said.

The Ragdoll nodded her head as though she resigned herself to the fact that this was her only option. I wanted to know who Lock Jaw was. Whoever, he or she was, I didn't like the name. He didn't sound like a cat. Cats jaws generally didn't lock, unless they'd been wired shut. How could a cat like that be beneficial to us?

I started to feel a little overwhelmed, a little like I was losing control with all the new tuna. I was a cat who liked to keep things simple and liked to know the cats that I worked with, to know exactly who they were. That was the only way that I was ever going to trust them and establish loyalty. I wasn't sure whether I wanted to have this Lock Jaw on my side, especially not if he was unpredictable. I found it challenging to trust cats straight away anyway, reaching out to the Ragdoll and Full Moon was a stretch. I admired Full Moon, but I wasn't too sure how I felt about the Ragdoll. There was too little that I knew about her.

"Whose land is this?" I asked.

I stopped. I wasn't going to walk a step further, until I had the time to process all of this new tuna. We no longer had to worry about the time. I couldn't do that until I knew where I was heading.

"We don't have time," the Ragdoll said.

"We have plenty of time," I said. "One Fang is already on Skinny's land."

"The Stables belong to Sahara. She'll need to know that One Fang has declared war on Skinny's land, which means that there'll be a war on the Neighbourhood. We can't have the Neighbourhood in a state of disarray," the Ragdoll explained.

I suddenly felt fiercely loyal. I continued to walk across the field. The Stables looked like another world. Whoever Sahara was, she had some fantastic territory. I thought that the Ragdoll's land was swish, but it paled in comparison.

The Stables was surrounded by acres of land; it was further than the eye could see. I recognised Jet and Ebony, who sat guarding the fence. I was a little taken aback by her presence. I wasn't expecting to see her there and didn't keep tabs on her. I never asked Stripes to watch her. Nothing she did seemed interesting.

Jet pressed the button and the gate began to open. The Bengal awaited our arrival. I followed the Ragdoll and Full Moon inside. Jet pressed the button to close the gate. That was some technology. I realised that the Bengal was Sahara.

"Autumn told me about Patches. I've sent Lock Jaw to seek him out. I imagine that he'll be licking his wounds," Sahara said. "Inspector White Tip, I understand you gave him quite a scratch."

"He'll be licking them even more after Lock Jaw has finished with him," Full Moon spat.

I began to wonder whether we were going to continue having our conversation on the forecourt, or if we were going to go somewhere private, when the Bengal led us inside.

"I gave Lock Jaw very specific orders. I made sure that he was fed before I sent for him, so that he wasn't tempted to eat him," Sahara said.

Full Moon looked furious. I knew that he was fiercely protective of the Ragdoll. I knew that I wanted him as another whisperer, but I had no idea if he worked for anyone else. He was loyal to the Ragdoll. It didn't mean that he'd be loyal to me. Most cats were only whisperers for one cat. I respected his loyalty. He was also a very good guard.

"Who is Lock Jaw?" I asked.

"He's the reason for my docked tail," Full Moon said.

"Lock Jaw and Full Moon lived with the same humans. Lock Jaw's human purchased Full Moon, only they never intended to have a cat for long. Instead, they used Full Moon for bait," Sahara explained.

Bait? Cats weren't cannibals. That meant that Lock Jaw had to be something else. I knew before she said it.

"Lock Jaw is a dog, who was trained for dog fighting," Sahara confirmed.

A dog! I barely trusted cats. There was no way that I would trust a dog, especially not a dog who was used for fighting.

Too right he was unpredictable. They were trained to attack. Cats were used as bait to frustrate them.

"How did you escape?" I asked.

"I scarpered up the wall and made my escape," Full Moon said.

Knowing how Full Moon lost his tail, made me wince even more. The pain was unimaginable. It was rare that cats had this. I'd never seen a cat with a skinned tail before. I wasn't sure how I'd ever forgive an animal for that. I needed to know how he was able to do it.

"How did you forgive him?" I asked.

"My mother presented me to her humans, and they had Lock Jaw removed. I forgave him the minute I saw him. He paid the ultimate price for letting me escape," Full Moon said. "They took his ears."

I felt sick to my stomach. Humans could be cruel, but that was vile. The more I heard from Full Moon, the more I realised how much I respected him. He was honourable for not seeking out revenge. It took true courage to be able to forgive.

As I looked down at the Neighbourhood. I used to think that Stripes had the best viewing spot. I thought she could see everything, but she barely had anything. From the vast windows, we could see everything that was happening. The whole Neighbourhood was within sight. The cats walked about like tiny rodents. If I'd not known who they were, I would've pounced at the windows to catch them. For a moment, I was in awe, then realisation took hold.

"You knew!" I shouted.

Normally, I would've been more respectful. I was in the presence of a pedigree cat, a member of the Cat Council and a lady of honour, but I couldn't hold back my indignation.

The Ragdoll looked on in horror. I felt her scorn. How dare a common house cat speak to a pedigree like that? Airs and graces meant nothing when faced with betrayal. Disloyalty always riled me up. If I was going to work with any of them,

I needed to trust them. How could I trust them if they kept secrets?

Sahara merely smiled smugly. What was I going to do? I was a common house cat, up at the Stables, without an ally. I'd been stupid. She had cats and even an unpredictable dog at her whim. I had two cats, who loyal as they were, were no match for a Bengal. If she chose to fight me, there was little chance that I would win. She was nearly the size of a lynx.

Then again, with the cats in her power, she didn't have to fight me. She was able to sit back and enjoy the entertainment.

"It took you a while Inspector White Tip, but you got there in the end," she added, smugly.

Full Moon walked to the window. Some of my faith was restored. At least he wasn't aware of the plan. Then, the Ragdoll walked over to the window to join me. She saw for herself, and the look of horror on her face deepened. She shook her head from side-to-side. She knew that Sahara had betrayed the trust of the Council and the entire Neighbourhood. The Ragdoll sat back. I couldn't tell whether or not it was because she felt betrayed or because she was choosing to be ignorant in the face of pride. She'd trusted the Bengal, and now she had a decision to make.

It was tough. I knew that the Ragdoll wasn't used to making decisions. She was a follower, a yes-cat. She always did what other cats expected of her. That was useful for any leader. After a while, being relentlessly challenged can become a bit of a tiresome battle. The Ragdoll was the perfect cat to have on one's side. Sahara needed her, but she needed not show it.

"Dolly, I asked Ebony to inform Graphite that we were waiting. Can you find out what's going on?" Sahara said.

The ragdoll bowed her head on exit. She called Full Moon to follow. The Bengal's cunning was as glossy as her fur. Dolly wasn't a servant; she was a pedigree. She deserved to be treated as an equal, yet she didn't cause a stir. Dolly was dutiful. I had to give her that.

Sahara waited until the door closed. Her teeth and collar gleamed in the moonlight. It was every bit as menacing as she intended it to be. I gave her the platform to begin.

"Inspector White Tip, I've been watching this Neighbourhood for years. I see the comings and the goings. I know that you care not for Mr One Fang. As far as I can see, this presents a perfect resolution for you because I'm the only one who can grant a locked-in order and have Mr One Fang removed, for good," Sahara said.

Nothing she said was untrue. I hated One Fang. I did want him removed from the streets. I thought it unfair that he'd taken ownership of Skinny Hind's land when there was no confirmation that Skinny Hind was gone forever. This was the perfect solution. Sahara had the resources. All I needed to do was say yes. He would've done the same to me, a million times over. He'd disobeyed the Council's order. We were here to bring about this exact situation, but it was too easy.

"Besides, the land really ought to go to yourself. Skinny would want it that way for his return. One Fang has broken an order," Sahara said.

"If you're going to give him the Order, don't let me stand in your way," I said.

"Now Inspector White Tip, let's not get stubborn. I know that you've had your whiskers pushed out of joint and you're a very loyal member of the Neighbourhood," Sahara said.

"If you knew, why didn't you place the order yourself?" I asked.

"I wanted to meet with you personally because the Council was most impressed by you. There's some discussion about there being an opening just for you. Wouldn't that be wonderful?" She said.

Graphite

# 13

## GRAPHITE

Cats on the Council lived the best lives. They have to make big decisions and were treated like kings and queens. Other cats rarely bothered them, except for the biggest issues. Winning a seat on the Council without being a pedigree cat was a pretty big deal. I could really see myself up there, giving my paw print of approval. Opportunities like this didn't come up often, and I wanted to grab it with all four of my paws. Curly Whiskers and Stripes would be instantly impressed. It'd improve all of our lives.

What about Skinny Hind? I realised that the Council used the permission to be on the Skittle Twins' land against me. They initially told me I was trespassing, which meant that when Skinny Hind returned, he would be trespassing on my land. What sort of move was that? It wasn't a good one. The integrity of the rules all about ensuring every cat had protection, and, without exception, their land was theirs if they lived there with their human.

When the British Short Hair arrived, I was quiet. I had a lot to contemplate, from immediate victory to guilt. Dolly and Full Moon walked in silently. Something about their silence reassured me that we all thought the British Short Hair was a flea.

"Sahara, my queen, how are we?" He said when he walked in. "Oh dear, I didn't realise that we were entertaining the common cats tonight."

Sahara beamed as soon as she saw him. She barely noticed the insult, until she saw my face. Then, she quickly corrected herself.

"Now, Graphite, I told Inspector White Tip about our earlier discussion," Sahara said.

I studied Graphite carefully. His amber eyes looked shifty. I could tell that he was wracking his brain to remember the discussion, and I knew why. No such discussion had taken place. I wasn't angry though. No, I wanted to play Sahara at her own game. I wanted to be entertained. I wondered what performance I would see. Was she going to be the lead and Graphite the nodding dog, or was he able to improvise? He was a bully, but was he intelligent enough to run with a story?

"Ah, yes, now I remember. It was about…" Graphite began.

I wondered how long the charade was going to go on for. It was like watching a mouse dance under the paw, as he waited for Sahara to rescue him. She left him there for a while. A part of me still thinks that she enjoyed that. It was her entertainment too, watching cats feeling intimidated by her with nowhere to run or hide. She was a bully.

"It was about Inspector White Tip joining the Council," Sahara finally said.

When he opened his amber eyes opened wide, his eyebrows disappeared into his fur. He looked horrified. He tried to compose himself.

"I wasn't aware that Inspector White Tip was a pedigree," Graphite said.

"Oh, I'm not," I said, with delight.

"Well, those paws they must be Maine Coon," Sahara said.

"They're not," I replied.

I enjoyed watching the wool unravel. There was no way that she was going to be able to save herself now. I wasn't a pedigree, but she surely couldn't rescind her offer. That'd be cruel.

"How long have you lived in the Neighbourhood now, Inspector White Tip, seven years?" Sahara asked.

"Three," I replied.

I wasn't about to help either of them. Graphite had no idea about the conversation. I knew that much. He wasn't pleased at all. It meant that he'd have to sit with one of the *common cats*.

"Sahara, darling, I think that we need to have a little chat," Graphite whispered.

"Yes, darling, I think you might be right," she said.

The two of them disappeared up the ladder onto the balcony above. I wondered how the pair of them were going to explain themselves out of this situation.

The silence of the room made it more obvious that they hadn't discussed the matter earlier. I suddenly realised that Sahara wasn't as powerful as she liked to make out. She was the front cat, instructed by Graphite. Graphite was clever enough to make her think that she had the power to do what she liked, and I saw that until now, she'd never really exercised it. That was how he made sure that he remained in power, by presenting her as the decision maker. It was clever, really. She was tall, she stood out, and was the distraction, whilst he did whatever he wanted. It took the spotlight off him. It was the work of a master scammer.

Sahara walked down looking timid. Graphite kept up his big smile. He'd sorted everything. She was going to be the star again. He was going to fix this little mistake of hers. I wondered what he said to her to make her so scared.

"Congratulations, Inspector White Tip. I believe you're our newest member," Dolly said with a warm smile, as soon as she saw them approaching.

I bowed my head in gratitude. I'd vastly underestimated her power. How clever to present herself as dutiful! She knew when to speak at the precise moment. I could tell that Dolly and Full Moon were enjoying the show as much as I was. I was pleased that she chose instinct above pride. I saw that wasn't a common practice around this part of the Neighbourhood.

Graphite scowled. He wasn't expecting that Dolly would betray him. He relied on her silence. Surely, Dolly knew that there was no place on the Council for a common house cat, yet she ignored it. She didn't trust Sahara or Graphite, and I liked that. She gave them enough floor to speak, but then, just when she needed to, she spoke, letting them live with their decisions.

"Inspector White Tip, Dolly, I think there has been some confusion. I was under the impression that we were speaking with a pedigree, or at the very least a pedigree's descendent. The Council only discussed whether or not there was a spot, and without lineage, a cat can't be a member," Sahara said.

The problem with Sahara was that she was never prepared. She was placed onto the pedestal early, and she believed that it was her entitlement to be there. Only, she never knew all of the rules. She accepted advice from other cats on the panel, but her own vanity marred her vision of morality. She had no more power than I did. Graphite and whomever else wanted it, did.

Graphite smiled smugly. Sahara had done what she was instructed to do. She had made a mistake, but rather than exercise her authority, she went back on her decisions, making her indecisive. It was a clever way of making her look incompetent.

"We are so sorry that Sahara raised your hopes like that. I know it must be disappointing," Graphite said.

I nodded my head. It was a clever distraction to pretend that I had a position on the Council. Meanwhile, I wasn't thinking about the Council's failure to impose a locked-in order on One Fang.

It was obvious that not all members were privy to Sahara's plan. It was dangerous for the Council to behave that way.

They should've been the utmost role models of loyalty, yet they were more fragmented than any of us in the Neighbourhood.

Full Moon sat silently. Dolly stared at the moon. Something told me that she was avoiding looking at the situation because she didn't approve. She wasn't about to be a part of the whole charade and was hiding something. Suddenly, she nodded at Full Moon, and he left the Stables. I wished I was excused. My time was being wasted. I should've been meeting with the other cats, building my army ready to overthrow One Fang's gang. It seemed obvious that Sahara had no intention to call a meeting to issue a locked-in order. If I was going to restore Skinny's land back to him, I needed time to act and fast. Instead, I wasted my time there, whilst One Fang was most probably preparing his cats for the biggest cat fight that there'd ever been in the Neighbourhood. Even if Patches was gone, One Fang had to suspect that something was wrong when he was missing. He'd only been sent to intimidate Dolly.

"Are we going to call a meeting?" Dolly asked.

"A meeting? What for?" Graphite meowed.

He was starting to really make my fur stand on edge. I'd respected the Council for a long time, but this Council was amok with false loyalties. How did they get anything done when all they were concerned with was conceited power?

"We have to have a vote for Inspector White Tip to be elected," Dolly said.

"Dolly, didn't you hear what Sahara said? Inspector White Tip isn't of pedigree lineage, so he cannot be a member," Graphite said with a yawn.

"The second amendment of the Feline Democratic Constitution states that we must have a vote to elect or decline a member of Council, if such a cat is not a cat of pedigree lineage," Dolly said.

I have to admit that my knowledge of the Council's rules at that point was sketchy. I'd never before considered being a member and had napping to catch up on, so I didn't make it my business to ensure that I knew all of the rules. I was busy enough investigating things like my land and didn't need the added responsibility of being a member of the Council. These days, I still don't need the responsibility, but I make it my business to ensure that I know all of the rules, just in case other cats think they can other throw the customs of the Council.

"Dolly, it was merely a suggestion; nothing was set in stone," Sahara scolded, she nodded at Graphite. She believed that everything was settled.

I wasn't a fan of the way she delegated her faults to other people. It was underhand. She was like a smiling assassin. She scolded whilst smiling. It was a good way of making another cat feel responsible, as though she forgave them for their misunderstanding.

"Oh, but Full Moon has just been to inform the rest of the Council that a meeting will commence within the hour. There'll be no way of informing him now. Autumn will be doing the same. You know how they are. They have an entire network that none of us are a part of," Dolly said.

I couldn't have been prouder. I expected Dolly to apologise and back down. She wasn't smiling, which made it sweeter.

Sahara looked at Graphite, who could only glare back. I saw that neither of them expected Dolly to fight back. Silently, Sahara marched in front of Dolly, as though she were prey. She sat straight in front of her, leaving Dolly with no option but to look up at her. I imagine that it was uncomfortable. Dolly craned her neck but showed no signs of discomfort.

"Dolly, who's in charge?" Sahara said.

"You hold the chair, but we all form the Council," Dolly said.

I respected her courage. Sahara was tall and looked particularly menacing with the way the light shone satanically around her head, casting dark, vicious shadows on the walls. She looked like she arrived with her own army. I knew that it would've taken an awful lot of inner strength to stand up to her. There was no doubt that Graphite was going to back Sahara to the hilt, regardless of how ridiculous the deed was going to be. Of course he was, he orchestrated it to be that way.

Sahara, who was somewhat taken aback by Dolly standing up to her, gulped. She had nothing to say and needed Graphite because she would've never reprimanded Dolly if it wasn't for him. She respected her because she knew that Dolly knew far more than she did.

Graphite joined Sahara's side. I was pleased that she had the decency not to smile; it was becoming a chore to witness. He looked livid. He wasn't used to Dolly challenging him. I could tell that much. He was fairly easy to read.

Graphite was another version of One Fang, except he looked down on the rest of us with contempt. Obviously, he believed we were dispensable by the way he cast me aside before considering me for the Council. He truly believed that only pedigree cats should sit on the Council, which might have been a long-standing custom, but things change. Some cats believed pedigrees were superior to all cats, just because of their lineage. I could name plenty of examples of cats who couldn't hold their own in a fight or even hunt for themselves and were humbled by circumstances. Sphinx was of course one of them, but there were far more than him I knew about. I think it was about that point when I realised that I actually preferred One Fang to Graphite.

I made sure I sat next to Dolly to show that she had support. Sahara and Graphite were more than able to summon a lot more cats than Dolly or me at that present moment, but she needed another cat in case she was willing to back down. There was a far bigger issue I wasn't privy to. I had no idea what I was letting myself in for, but I knew when it came to choosing sides that I'd always choose Dolly.

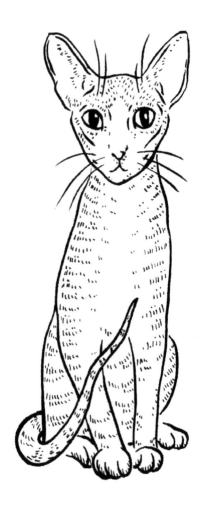

Crinkles

*Lock Jaw*

# 14

## THE BEST OF FRIENDS

"Dolly, think about what you are doing. This isn't a wise decision," Graphite warned.

Graphite's eyebrows furrowed. His lips were thin. His chin tucked into his chest. He wasn't about to back down. He was ready for what came his way.

Sahara looked pained. Common cats were easy to dismiss, but cats of the Council, they were a select group. They were trusted with the knowledge of things happening in the Neighbourhood. They were supposed to be informed of everything, to ensure that there was balance. They cared little for generic land fights, but they knew of the bigger issues. They were cats who came together. They had their own team of cats that they led, and these went into the wider network of whisperers and watchers, and then onto the rest of us.

"I don't need to be patronised. I know the weight of my decision. I've thought about it. The Council needs to be aware that there is a power play occurring here," Dolly said.

"A power play? No. Dolly, this was a mistake that you mistook for being an agenda. Once the other cats arrive, well, this will all be put to rest," Graphite said.

Sahara walked off. Graphite followed, leaving behind a mound of grey fur. If this were a fight for territory, Dolly would've won this round because she'd sat it out; they left.

However, this wasn't a simple land fight. I had no idea what I was actually supporting. I just had to show up.

When the other members began to show up, I started to feel nervous. I wasn't a member, and there was no obvious reason for me to be there. They could've easily dismissed me, as Graphite had when I arrived, but there were lots of them. Most of them were pedigree cats. I stuck out, and it felt a little uncomfortable. My fur felt as though it needed a cleaning. These cats were well-groomed, probably several times a day. They ate well. I felt as though I'd rolled in the mud beforehand. My fur was in nowhere near as good a condition.

"Where do you want us Dolly?" the Cornish Rex said.

"Crinkles, take a seat wherever you want," Dolly said.

I was impressive that they knew that Dolly would be hosting. I thought they would've asked for Sahara, as the chair. We were on her land. I realised that I needed to improve my communication with both Stripes and Curly. Full Moon and Dolly knew what was needed without speaking.

I was mesmerised by the number of pedigree cats that were in the Neighbourhood. I was sure that I hadn't seen many of them at the trial. I had no idea how Full Moon had managed to gather so many of them in the short time that he had. Pedigree cats were rarely seen in the Neighbourhood because they had precise routines. How they managed to convince their humans to allow them to attend the meeting, I'll never know.

Sahara looked emotional as she came down from the balcony. She bowed her head and appeared grateful to have Graphite by her side. Sahara knew that she'd done something wrong, and there was no way to get out of it. She wasn't as clued up on the rules as Dolly was. She felt betrayed – cats didn't question the chair, and Graphite looked furious. He nodded at Sahara, supporting her. She took her seat on the floor, and Graphite joined the crowd.

"My fellow members, respected member, Dolly the Third, has called us here today over a matter of a power play," Crinkles said.

The room was full of cats whispering amongst themselves. She later told me that she'd sent the message via cat code. She knew that some of the cats were less informed about the rules, but when she'd asked Jet and Ebony to deliver the message six, Crinkles knew exactly what that meant. He was a stickler for rules.

Crinkles was an unusual looking cat. His ears were long, and his head was large. His whiskers curled at the ends, unlike Curly, whose whiskers were almost coiled. I would've noticed Crinkles around the Neighbourhood because of his looks. He was tall and well-groomed. The white in his fur was so pure; it looked brand new. The sandy brown waves in his fur rippled in patches. He was most definitely a house cat the majority of the time. I was sure of it.

"One Fang has acted within the face of the Council and has taken occupation over Skinny Hind's land," Dolly said. "As you can see, by looking through the window, there is a perfect view of the Neighbourhood. We can see that One Fang and Old Ginger Paws are currently sat on his land."

Some of the cats took their opportunity to corroborate what Dolly was saying and turned to nod at the rest of the Council.

"Sahara?" Crinkles asked.

"Well, I don't spend my time looking down at the Neighbourhood. I've other matters to attend to," she lied.

I wasn't surprised that she lied. After all, I was used to seeing Sahara and Graphite promising one thing and delivering the opposite. Those two acted for themselves without forethought for the rest of the Neighbourhood. I wasn't angry. Dolly witnessed it. It was enough to make her call a meeting.

"As chair, Sahara it's your responsibility to ensure that the Neighbourhood is operating as it should. You admitted to Inspector White Tip that you'd seen he was there. You failed to act upon it. You're in violation of the Neighbourhood Act." Dolly said.

I wondered how a chair had their chair removed. A chairperson made the final decision on nearly everything that happened in the Neighbourhood.

"Sahara admitted to me that she only noticed One Fang's presence on the land, mere minutes before Inspector White Tip arrived. She had no time to call a meeting," Graphite explained.

"Sahara can speak for herself," Crinkles said.

I was pleased to see Graphite quiet for the first time that evening. He wasn't going to challenge any of the cats there. It wouldn't look good. It meant that Sahara had to answer for herself. I was glad that none of the cats felt intimidated by her. It was a lot easier to go against her in large numbers than being alone. Now, she looked like a meek kitten.

"Are you acting on behalf of One Fang?" Dolly asked.

"Of course not. One Fang has gone against our decision and taken occupation of Skinny Hind's land. I intended to have him arrested," Sahara said.

Crinkles looked around, confused.

"Where is Lock Jaw?" Crinkles asked.

"Lock Jaw was sent to collect Patches. Patches attempted to attack me tonight on my own land," Dolly said. "He hasn't returned yet."

In all of the excitement, I'd forgotten that Lock Jaw hadn't returned with Patches. My stomach began to churn. Something was wrong. Graphite looked pretty pleased with himself. He had to have intercepted the message to Lock Jaw. Lock Jaw was trained to sprint and ensure that Patches didn't escape.

I was pretty confident that Patches would know who he was – he was streetwise. He knew nearly everything going on in the Neighbourhood, if not more. Patches would've been a good whisperer to have if he could keep himself controlled. His wily nature was too much for me. He was as unpredictable as Lock Jaw.

I once witnessed Patches wait for a car that had nearly caught his tail by speeding along the road. He sat in the same spot, not sleeping for days. When he saw the car, he leapt onto the bonnet, hissed and caused the car to collide with another. The human got out of the car, screaming and shouting. Patches swiped at his legs before running off into the distance. The human, terrified, climbed back into their car quickly and drove off into the distance.

"Jet and Ebony you need to search for them. They should be here now," Crinkles said.

Jet and Ebony nodded at him. Crinkles searched around, looking under the furniture and then into the crowd.

"Has One Fang not been sent for?" Crinkles asked.

"They couldn't find him," Graphite lied.

I was beginning to become suspicious. Graphite looked as though he was protecting One Fang. He knew as well as I did, that he should've had him arrested immediately. There was something that he and Sahara were hiding.

"Would he not be on Skinny Hind's land?" Crinkles asked.

Graphite seemed to play the fool. He had an ah-ha moment and smacked his head with his paw. It was obvious where One Fang was. A dog could've thought of that.

"I'm going to suggest that we allow One Fang to occupy the land a little longer, so that we have evidence when we summon him," Crinkles said. "Am I correct that Skinny Hind hasn't yet been found?"

"No he hasn't," Dolly replied.

"We only have a matter of hours before the land becomes free now anyway, so I'm going to agree with Sahara to not arrest him for the time being. Graphite, I want you to inform One Fang that the land will be need to be vacated within the next few hours for the waiting list," Crinkles said.

Dolly looked at me. She knew that something wasn't right. One Fang should've been arrested for violating the code. That was what usually happened. If anything, the land had to be vacated for longer because of the lack of respect for the original order. I knew that much. He disrespected a Council decision and should've been locked-in.

"Patches will need to be detained. No cat should have to protect themselves on their own land, especially not a member of the Cat Council. Is there any cat who has space?" Crinkles said.

None of it made sense. They were going to place a locked-in order on Patches, but not One Fang. *What made him so special?* Crinkles thought no cat should have to protect themselves on their own land. There was no proof that Skinny wasn't going to return.

"Why will he not be sent here?" Sahara asked, confused.

I looked around the Stables there was plenty of room to detain many of the cats with and without humans. It seemed like the perfect spot to detain Patches. I wasn't sure that any of the cats would've given some of their land to house a locked-in cat, especially not Patches. I wasn't surprised when none of the cats volunteered their land.

Patches would fight the whole time he was there because he was a street cat. He had spent very little time in the company of humans because he was accustomed to fighting for his survival and freedom; I think he was abandoned by humans when he was a kitten. Patches wasn't going to accept being locked-in easily.

The rest of the cats seemed to ignore Sahara's question. Even Graphite avoided eye contact.

"Why will he not be sent here?" Sahara repeated.

"You can't be trusted," Graphite eventually said.

That was the reason why he chose not to sit with her! Sahara was wounded. She could've handled the news from another cat. She couldn't handle the news from a cat that she thought was her friend. She immediately knew that Graphite was no longer on her side. She never expected that he'd drop her so quickly. Graphite switched sides. He knew that Sahara was no longer powerful. I almost felt sorry for her, but it was hard to feel empathy for a cat who was willing to tread on the paws of other cats to gain more power. Skinny was going to return to his human's land, having to fight back for his occupation, I couldn't feel empathy for her. She didn't deserve any cat's trust.

"We're going to have to use Sahara's land to detain him, and if he acts up again, he will have to be banished from the Neighbourhood," Dolly said.

I wouldn't have offered my land up for Patches either.

When Jet and Ebony returned, I knew that they'd had a hard time controlling Lock Jaw. Their fur looked worn, and they were both panting. Lock Jaw was the size of a horse. He towered over the room. Some cats shrank back in fear, which probably antagonised him even more. Patches legs were flailing, and drool drenched his coat. I could tell that he wasn't happy. What cat would be when they'd been in the company of a dog?

The large, red beast set him down on the floor. I thought he was going to scarper straight away. He didn't dare. He looked completely defeated. There were spots of blood in his fur. Patches hadn't been taken without a fight though; there were scratches around Lock Jaw's mouth. It must have taken a lot of will power not to rip something apart when it was attacking you.

Crinkles nodded at a reddish-coloured, Somali cat. Her tail was bushy, like a fox's. From behind, it would've been an easy mistake to make, but her face was more petite, almost gentle-looking. She opened the door and dragged out a pheasant. I would never know who'd caught that thing. It was colossal and looked fresh too. She dragged it to Lock Jaw's feet with ease, showing her incredible strength.

"Thank you Autumn," Lock Jaw said, before turning around and tearing into it. Some of its bones snapped as Lock Jaw bit into it. Even Patches shook a little. That could've been him.

Autumn, I'd heard that name before. She was one of the watchers. If she could hunt too, then that made her a weapon. It occurred to me that she probably lived free. It was the only way that she could be so aware of all of the tuna, yet her fur was so well-maintained, that it had to be brushed.

"Scrawny Patches, you are sentenced to a locked-in order for seventy-two hours for the unreasonable attack of a Council Cat on her own land," Crinkles said.

There was no summons, no trial, no discussion. When a cat attacked another on their human's land, they were instantly sentenced.

Patches simply shrugged his shoulders. I expected more of a reaction than that. He almost looked pleased with himself. He nodded his head, dutifully, almost remorsefully. It had to be another of One Fang's tricks, to try and get some more inside tuna. I wanted to question him.

Jet and Ebony led Patches to his stable for the night. I followed him in.

"I need to question him," I said.

"You have five minutes," Jet said.

They closed the door. It didn't look like a shabby deal with a bed in the stable and some food in there. Though it wasn't homely, but it had to be easier than being on the streets.

"Inspector White Tip, if I'd have known you were going to be here I'd have cleaned up a bit," Patches said. He scratched his nails into the floor. It made a horrible sound because the wood had been treated. I suspected that he tore a claw or two as he struggled to pull his claws from it.

"You'd need more than a claw file," I said.

Patches sniffed at that. He gave a good fight even when he'd lost a life and was down on his luck.

"Well I can do all the cleaning up I need to in here," he said bitterly.

"Then what?" I asked.

"What do you mean?" He said, incredulous to the accusation that he'd be doing anything else other than going about his business in the Neighbourhood.

I wasn't fooled. Patches had a lot of time to fill. He had all the freedom in the world. He was too wily to sleep. I'd be surprised if he slept sixteen hours a day. He didn't have humans to keep him company. He smelt of more than only Lock Jaw's drool.

"I got me a big piece of land," Patches boasted.

"Oh, and where's that then?" I asked.

"You should know it. It's got a lovely pond, a nice tree in it. You kept the other cats away. I suppose I owe you a thank you," he said.

"Skinny isn't dead. He's very much alive, and when he returns, that land will be rightfully returned to him," I said.

I hated the way some of the Neighbourhood treated Skinny's disappearance as death. There was no grace period for him. He'd only been gone a matter of days, and trespassers riddled the place.

"That cat crossed rainbow bridge five days ago," Patches said.

Patches walked around me, his tail swishing this way and that as though he were transferring his scent to me. The smell hit my nostrils hard. He didn't need to be near me. His scent was already on me from the other side of the door, so this was just to rile me up.

"If he has, there's no way that you're getting that land. One Fang has wanted it for too long," I advised.

"Well, he promised it to me," Patches said.

It surprised me that Patches was even considering settling into human territory. He liked to be out in the dark hours and to come and go as he pleased. Patches wore the au naturel as a badge of honour.

For me, life was easier with humans. Cats didn't have to fret about food or sleep, but they had to abide by the rules.

They had to go outside when they were instructed to. If they missed the let in time, then that was it, they were out for the night in the elements. They dialled into their instincts for cats, prey, foxes, and cars. It was fun at first, and then, it soon became miserable, especially when the weather was anything other than dry. I hated washing my fur after it rained because it tasted funny. But for Patches, this was the dream. He liked to be in charge of himself.

"You're going to live with humans?" I asked, sceptical.

"No. I don't have to live with the humans. I can live off the fish and the birds," Patches said.

"What do you think happens when you finish the fish? The humans won't keep replacing them. What about when the birds have had one or two disappear from the nest?" I said.

"They'll keep away. They're only there at the minute because Skinny isn't hunting them. He doesn't need to. The humans are feeding him."

Patches looked annoyed. He had to know I was speaking the truth. The fish in the pond belonged to the humans too. Skinny knew to respect that. The sparrows wouldn't be there forever if their young were at risk. Patches, One Fang and any other cat who looked at Skinny's land as a bountiful paradise had to realise that there was a time limit on that if they were going to hunt there.

"Why do you care then?" Patches said.

"Loyalty. Honour. A cat deserves to return to their land and know that they don't have to fight for it. We all know that." I said.

He sat down, impressed. I had no reason to lie to him. It mattered to me that cats held up the Feline Foundations. It protected us all.

"What good is it when you're in here?" I asked. "One Fang isn't fighting for you to have the land. He's just ensured that another cat doesn't get it. That's why you're in here, and he's over there."

Patches curled up in a ball. He looked like a forlorn kitten. For a minute, I thought he actually might have been crying. His eyes were huge and his fur looked mangy. I walked over to the food bowl. Cat biscuits! Cardboard would have been tastier, especially for a hunter. Either way, I nudged the bowl towards him.

"You know; human companions aren't that bad. They can turn out to be pretty handy, especially when it's cold and raining," I said.

Patches nodded miserably. I felt a little sorry for him. I'd once been in his paw prints before I found the Duchess and the Male One.

It'd been a lonely year. My humans left without waiting for me. I wandered the streets lonely and hungry. Then, I thought I found humans, but the humans wanted me to befriend the other cats that lived there. I just couldn't.

Hairball was forever coughing up a fur ball. It was the only exercise he got. He lay most of the day in the cat bed, taking up all of the space. Then he'd wake up, coughing and spluttering for ages, until finally this huge fur ball came up. He'd then go back to bed, snoring loudly. I've no idea how he ever had fur balls. He was always either sleeping or eating.

There was Molly as well. Her name was short for Molly Coddles because that was all she did, fuss about everything. At first it was endearing, but it soon became annoying, especially with the lack of sleep. "White Tip, are you going to clean your fur? White Tip, have you cleaned behind your ears? White Tip, have you scratched your claws today? White Tip, have you eaten your food, or is that mine? White Tip, have you cleaned your paws? White Tip, are we going hunting? White Tip, where are you going?"

After a while, I hissed. The humans found me aggressive and took me to a horrific place. They put into a cage with barely any room. I had nothing and nowhere to scratch my claws. The other cats in the room would meow incessantly about how awful it was. The situation wasn't changing any time soon. Then, when the humans came into the room they'd be meowing like crazy, begging to be chosen to go home with them. I didn't bother. I was older than most of them in there.

Then, one day, the Duchess and the Male One walked into the room. My claws were long and dangled outside of the cage. The Male One had the audacity to stroke my paws whilst I tried to sleep. The Duchess had far more respect for me.

They took me home, and for a while, I had to learn how to follow human rules again. I thought I could have total freedom, and took my shot at it. It was Summer, so the weather was decent. Then, after a lot of territory fights, I was hungry and had to go back to my human's land. I liked the regularity of food and sleep. I preferred these humans to the last set.

"I'm going to let you get your rest. You've been through a lot," I said. "Anytime, you want to know what it's like to live with decent humans, give me a call."

"White Tip, watch out for the Short Hair. He's a good friend of One Fang's," Patches said.

I appreciated the tip off for many reasons, petty and proper. I truly believed that Patches wanted to settle down. I knew places where he would actually feel like he belonged. One Fang had used him and then dispensed of him. I knew what he was like, but for Patches to show emotion, that had to mean something.

When I left his room, the Council had departed. I crept through the dark stable and got the fright of my life, when I saw Lock Jaw lay on the ground! Fortunately, he was asleep, but I still had to be careful.

# 15

## A CHANGE OF FOCUS

The walk back from the Stables was a little hairy. I knew that it'd be a while before the owls and foxes were out. After seeing the pheasant, I wasn't fancying my chances of coming across one. They were strong and usually travelled in large groups. They could cause a fair bit of damage in a fight, so I didn't really fancy having to fight one.

I felt a little inspired when I saw a hare in the distance. It'd been a while since I'd hunted one, but it was too far for me to chase. I longed for a rabbit to rear its head, but I had no such luck. Night had fully descended upon the Neighbourhood when I got there. Night was usually a cat's favourite time of the day. We could use our instincts and had almost total freedom. Dogs were usually finishing off their last walks, and humans went in cars or were inside, which made the Neighbourhood a playground.

At night, cats go onto the lands of dogs' because they're usually inside, or have specific times they're allowed out into their gardens. That means further areas to hunt and grab food. Mice quite often think they are safe in the residence of a dog's property, but that's only in the day.

One of my favourite areas to go, was a human's garden, who wasn't too fond of cats. The human was a keen gardener with a nasty temper. I'd seen him a few times, chase cats off his land with a spade or a rake a few times. The soil was always soft. When I saw him getting at the cats, I usually took my revenge by leaving him a present, partially buried in his garden.

Just that morning, the human had taken the liberty of having a go at the smallest human in my house, the Little Lady, for being too noisy. Humans think only dogs are territorial and will protect them, but that's because most dogs are on leads and can only react when they're with their humans. Cats are more cunning. We like to take our time, and not make it too obvious. I wanted to make a stop at the nasty-tempered one's house, to pay my respects.

As I spoke with Curly Whiskers, I watched as he planted some new flowers in the garden, raked over the soil to make sure no weeds took root, watered the flowers, then stood back and admired them. As he did that, the Duchess and the Male One walked past, which was when she laughed, and the nasty-tempered one shouted. I knew to remember to make a stop there.

As I pulled the new flowers from the garden, Curly Whiskers came over.

"White Tip, what are you doing? You're supposed to be making allies, not digging up flowers," Curly hissed.

"I've got my tuna. We just need to bide our time," I explained. "The Council will put in their order, but we need to wait a while. They're too divided at the moment," I said.

"Is this for the Little Lady?" Curly asked.

I didn't have to respond. We both knew that it was. Curly dug the rest of the flowers out. We made sure that it looked like the garden had moles in it, by leaving lots of little mounds.

"Brown Crown is not going to agree to work with us. He has a lot of tuna coming his way. The Skittle Twins aren't going to demand their land back, not now – it's overrun with his cats. They've taken residence on the three houses in every direction," Curly said.

I shrugged my shoulders. I wasn't surprised. I knew that One Fang was going to take as much as he could. Whatever it was about Skinny's land, he wanted it for himself, and he wasn't about to give it up. I couldn't understand why he wanted it so much. The food would disappear, and it'd be just like anyone else's land, eventually.

"The Bengal knew that he had the land," I said. "She knew, but allowed him to take residence anyway because One Fang has the Short Hair getting him all the power that he wants."

It was one of the only times I've ever seen Curly lost for words. He rarely reacted to any news. He just took it in his stride and thought about the next action, taking orders as he needed to.

"That's how he got the trial arranged. Patches told me that One Fang and Graphite are friends. Graphite instructed Sahara, the Bengal to do nothing," I explained.

Curly wasn't especially keen on Patches. Patches could be cruel, even to the cats who'd already dealt with a lot. It was hard to show empathy to a cat who didn't do the same. Even if he changed soon, some wounds take a lot longer to heal than others.

He wasn't shocked to know that the Council had let One Fang off. He was always sceptical of them. I liked to believe that they were there for good, but Curly thought that many of them had their own agendas. He couldn't accept that they were moral cats, when they didn't often let common cats in. He had a point.

I wanted to get on with finding Skinny. I was getting tired of cats giving up on him. They seemed to accept that he had walked across the rainbow bridge. I wondered if they'd be so relaxed if the Neighbourhood was comfortable with *their* disappearance.

"All we know is that he was carried out with a sheet covering him, and then he went to the vets. We don't have anything else to go on. Stripes was the only cat who saw it," Curly said.

"She couldn't have seen him," I said.

"Of course, she could. She has the best view of the Neighbourhood," Curly said.

I grew side-tracked. As I told him about Stripes' point not having visibility of Skinny's land, something changed in him. He was hurt, let down. Curly liked cats to be honest. I saw that he was angry at me too, for taking her word for it.

I knew that Curly would feel annoyed. I wanted to give him time to process the tuna before I stepped in with my own thoughts. Curly mulled over it for a few minutes. He tugged at the flowers and took way more than he needed to. He spat them out and kept going. I continued to watch; it was his way of processing his emotions.

"I'm not talking here. There are too many ears," he said and threw a quick glance up at Stripes.

I followed Curly to my eight o'clock cuddles. Sometimes, the humans left the shed door open.

Curly sat up straight. He wasn't too happy to still be working with Stripes. He felt betrayed by her. I could see why. She hadn't seen Skinny disappear. How did she even know that he was gone? She stood on trial, taking an oath, and lied.

I sat for a minute. That was a lot of action to take on one technicality. I trusted Stripes as much as I trusted Curly. It felt a little impulsive to just cut her loose. Stripes was an independent cat and didn't like lots of cats bothering her. She didn't have a wide network like Curly. I understood his anger; Stripes wasn't totally honest about what she saw. On that note, neither was I. I sat on that tuna. Did that mean that he was going to leave also?

I felt guilty for not telling him earlier. It should have been one of the first things that I told him, as soon as I knew. He seemed to take my withholding tuna a lot better than he took Stripes doing it.

"You should've told me, but you had your reasons. Stripes has none. She has no reason to be loyal to any of those other cats. She's a weak link acting on her emotions," Curly said.

"I think that's a little harsh. If we cut her loose, we're both acting on your emotions. Stripes had her reasons. She isn't acting for One Fang." I said.

"How do you know?" he asked.

"I know it in my gut. She despises One Fang as much as we do. There is no way that she would work for him. She barely likes working with us. Curly, I intend to find the reason for why she didn't tell me how she knew that Skinny was missing, but for now, it's not the important thing. Let's not be blindsided by our emotions," I said.

Curly combed his tail with his claws. He always did this whenever he felt angry. He knew that I was right. It was his form of sulking. I knew that I had to ask him something. There'd never been the right moment because something else always seemed to creep up.

"Why weren't you the first to tell me that Skinny Hind was missing?" I asked.

I tried to remain calm, but something in me knew that there was going to be a horrible surprise at the end of that question. Curly paused for a moment, then sat up bolt upright.

"The first I heard of it was when you told me," Curly said.

It was then that I realised the huge mistake. Curly was close to the ground. He had his network of whisperers. It made no sense that he wouldn't have known about Skinny Hind. Skinny was his student, his protégée. The first cat that anyone would have sought out, would have been Curly. They would've known what it meant to him.

"She said that he'd been missing for three days," I said, dumbfounded.

I had accepted that Stripes was upset that Skinny was missing. After all, Skinny was the only reason why she'd agreed to work with me. She never worked with anyone.

My insides churned. I'd defended her lies. Stripes had always told me everything in full detail, so I never questioned her, so it would've been so easy to get me to investigate this whole situation. She knew that I wouldn't have questioned her on anything. I would've accepted anything that she said.

"Just suppose that the cat who came to her wasn't One Fang. Who else would it have been?" Curly said.

I knew that the entirety of One Fang's gang would've been ruled out. She truly despised them, so it had to be another cat completely separate from his gang, who had their suspicions about the things happening there, or one who wanted to plant a seed. It had to be a cat who Stripes would've trusted. That was a difficult one because Stripes was aloof. She rarely bothered with any of the details of the Neighbourhood. Her usual news was to tell me about a cat who was about to or had trespassed on my land. My usual business was to have my land fights, and then I rewarded Stripes with something that I'd hunted.

"Who would she trust enough to take their word for it?" I asked.

Stripes didn't trust anyone. I realised that I'd never questioned why she cared so much about what happened to Skinny Hind. I accepted that she didn't want me to fight him because she thought he deserved a chance, but there had to be another reason, a bigger reason.

Stripes would've seen Curly training him, making sure that he knew how to handle himself. She would've known that Curly and I worked together, so I knew not to fight Skinny. Yet she begged me not to fight him. She said that was her condition.

There was Curly, Skinny, and me – those were the only cats that Stripes trusted. I tapped my claws on the floor whilst I contemplated who she would've spoken to. Then, it dawned on me. The reason why she cared so much had to be that she knew Skinny before he was thrown from the car. Her spot was good, but the streets were too far away to see; not even the Stables' view was that good.

# 16

## DIFFERENCES ASIDE

Stripes sat on the top of the roof, eyes narrowed, with a smile on her face. She looked totally at peace up there. Seeing her this way made me almost nostalgic for the simpler times when she only cared for looking out for my land. She yawned when I called her down to the lower roof.

"Where's my dinner?" She asked, shocked.

I had to try with all my might not to get angry. She was supposed to be on form and alert, checking out what was happening. She was supposed to be informing me of things that were happening in the Neighbourhood. Now wasn't the time for rest, though I too wanted it to be.

"You need to start giving me answers, without the reward of food," I hissed.

"What answers?" Stripes asked aggressively.

Stripes was like a sibling to me. I felt fiercely protective of her, but she irritated me to my core sometimes. She couldn't omit these details from me any longer. It wasn't fair. She had asked me to investigate Skinny's disappearance, so she needed to tell me why we were doing that. It had already cost me a lot.

"Stripes, I know that you didn't see Skinny leave. You couldn't have. His land is in your blind spot. I saw it when I was down there," I said, sticking my chin out.

Stripes broke her glare by lowering her head. She looked like a kitten. I almost was swayed by her vulnerability, but this was getting to be really serious. This meant fighting off One Fang and his powerful affiliations.

"We belonged to the same litter. We were the last two before the humans came for us. They wanted me at first, but I needed to know where Skinny had gone," She said through choked tears. "I needed to know that he'd find a home and be wanted. I bit one of them. They wanted him straight away."

"What happened to you?" I asked.

"My humans are inside. Our mother was put down because she was ill. I was heartbroken and climbed up here. I've never been inside since. Then, months passed, and I saw this skinny cat walking around the streets with our mother's markings. I knew it was him," she said.

I understood what she said. She felt responsible for his humans abandoning him. She had misguided guilt, but that didn't explain how she knew that he was missing.

"That doesn't explain how you knew that he was missing, *if* he was missing," I said bluntly.

I stood to leave. I wanted her to feel the urgency. She needed to tell us what we'd gotten ourselves into. She needed to me what all of this was for.

"He's missing. Jet told me," she said.

My heart sank. Jet wasn't a cat that I would trust. I wasn't sure whether or not she'd actually seen Skinny disappear. Her land was set back. It was near impossible to know what was going on two houses down, let alone all the way down to Skinny's land.

"Jet's been suspicious for a while. She saw that Sahara was only asserting power in certain parts of the Neighbourhood. She saw One Fang hanging around. Then, when she went to see what was happening," she explained.

Jet was athletic enough to climb up to Stripes' roof. She was inconspicuous enough not to be seen, especially if she climbed up at night. It would've been difficult to spot her even from the Stables. She was a black cat.

"How did she know he was missing?" I asked.

"She saw Skinny being carried out under a blanket," Stripes said glumly.

"Yet, you sit here comfortably basking in the moonlight?" I accused.

I knew I was being harsh, but I didn't want unfeeling cats working with me. I wanted cats who cared about other cats, not ones who sat back in the complacency that they'd done a little bit, and that was good enough. If she cared so much for Skinny Hind, she would've been desperate enough to climb down from her pedestal, and she'd demand answers from every cat in the Neighbourhood and me. That was how I reasoned it. It was uncharacteristic of her to be so insensitive.

"I sit and I don't bask. What would you rather, me constantly demanding what you know and getting in the way of your investigation? Then, you'd be accusing me of not trusting you," Stripes hissed.

Stripes was livid. I'd never seen her so affected by anything. Her fur stood on edge. She was small, but she was definitely intimidating.

"I put all of my trust in you White Tip," she continued.

"Why didn't you come to trial to support me instead of as a witness?" I said. I felt as though she should've been there, especially after she gave her statement. She stepped down from the stand, and that was it. It stung to be deserted by my own watcher.

"Do you know what they did to me?" Stripes hissed and began to step forwards.

I began to step back. Her ferocity stood like a force between us.

"No," I whispered.

My shame was strong. I knew that she looked dishevelled but stayed true to her word. I had an inkling that whatever it was, it was awful. She'd found me when I needed her, but I never presented myself when she needed me. I hadn't even asked her about it.

"One Fang bit me. I had an abscess and had to seek out my humans so that I could get checked out. Never question my loyalty, White Tip. I'm not here to be insulted," she added.

"I need you to tell me everything. You know the deal. It's no good telling me a bit of this and a bit of that. I agreed to do this for you. I never questioned why I was doing it. I accepted the job because you asked me to do it. I question your loyalty when you hold back tuna; it affects us all," I hissed back.

There was far more to say, but I was suddenly conscious of other cats about who could reach us. I don't know what it was, but the ground seemed to be too still when there was a breeze blowing through the Neighbourhood.

"The same could be said for you. You're not exactly an open book of tuna," Stripes said.

I had my reasons to be guarded with the tuna that I knew. She was an informant. Her job was to tell me what she knew. There was no reason to keep things from me. I made sure that she knew that. There was something that I needed to tell her though that she should know.

"Skinny is alive, but I've no idea where he is," I said. I knew she needed to have some hope.

"He is!" she beamed. "That's all we need to know for now."

I took her saying that as forgiveness. For a moment, I thought that she was going to drop me.

"You owe me a bird, not one of those sparrows though," Stripes said.

# 17

## CONTROVERSY

I hit my wall. I had few answers about Skinny. I was beginning to feel defeated by the whole thing. I didn't want to have to fight One Fang, I would end up seriously hurt, and there was no guarantee that Skinny was going to return home.

When I arrived back at my human home, Old Ginger Paws sat on the drive waiting for me. He was the last person that I wanted to see. I sprinted my way along the street. I expected him to at least stand up when he saw me, but he remained seated. I had to stop myself from colliding with him.

"Get off my land!" I hissed.

My back was arched; my claws were ready. I wasn't about to sacrifice my land to one of One Fang's gang. Old Ginger Paws curled himself up into a ball. He wrapped his tail around him. I couldn't understand why he remained sat there if he was scared. This wasn't a sink or swim situation. Sure, the Council was all over the place, but even if Graphite did take power, I'd still have right to my human's land.

"Why are you still here?" I hissed.

"I'm not leaving until you listen to me," Old Ginger Paws said.

"Listen to you. I don't have to listen to you. Nothing you have to say is of any relevance to me," I hissed.

Old Ginger Paws wasn't moving, but I knew he was scared. There was no point in me fighting him then, I was only going to tire myself out. It meant that all of his muscles were protected because they were tense. I resigned myself to listening to him.

"I'll listen, but you are to do this from the pavement," I said.

Old Ginger Paws uncurled himself and sat on the pavement, bordering my land. I waited until he was completely off before I sat down. He only had limited time anyway. The Male One's car was parked on the driveway. I knew as soon as he heard me hissing that it wouldn't be long until the Male One chased Old Ginger Paws off my land.

"I don't have long, so I'll make this quick. One Fang has disbanded most of us. He's working with Graphite now and he doesn't care who knows it," Ginger Paws said.

I had to admit, he sounded panicked. I wasn't fooled though. There was no bar for how low One Fang would go. I'd seen all of this before in the trial. This just sounded like another ploy to make the rest of the cats feel sorry for them and then he knew all of the tricks and plans to have him under a locked-in order. I yawned. It was so predictable. I didn't know why he bothered with these silly little games. He had the land. He'd won. No one was actually fighting him; not even the Council were bringing him down – much to my annoyance.

"White Tip, we need you. Shadows has headed over to speak to Curly Whiskers now. Skippy will be heading over to Stripes," Old Ginger Paw said.

I sat up, unbothered that they knew who my whisperer was. Curly could handle himself just fine. I'd seen him train cats to fight and hunt, he was able to handle himself no problem. It was Stripes that I worried about. She didn't deserve to have to fight off another of One Fang's gang. She'd already endured enough.

"Tell Skippy and any of the others to stay away from Stripes. You've already done enough damage," I hissed.

Old Ginger Paws seemed hurt that I wouldn't trust him. I just hoped that he wasn't stupid enough to think that I'd just accept something that came out of his mouth. His whiskers twitched, and so did mine.

"White Tip we need to go quickly. They're on their way," Old Ginger Paws warned.

I looked because there was no way that I'd trust him. The air seemed to change. I saw One Fang, Graphite and some of the others piercing eyes through the darkness. They were far enough away that we still had a lead.

"Follow me," I said.

The best thing to do when cats were descending on you, was to walk rather than run. Running indicated that you had something to hide. Whilst I expected One Fang and Graphite weren't the fittest cats in the world, I suspected that they had some more athletic cats in their group. He'd managed to persuade Patches to act on his behalf. We walked under the gate, over the fence, and through the ginnel because there was no way that we were taking refuge on my territory, and into the older humans' gardens.

I liked the older humans. Sometimes, I made it my business to stop by because they liked to make a fuss of cats. Some of them poured out milk or cream; some even bought fresh cuts of meat. Either way, it was usually a stop I made if I wanted endless pampering. I could spend hours and hours there.

My only issue with visiting the older humans was that there were usually many cats there, and I wasn't a fan of a lot of cats. One lady used to get very upset if we didn't all get along, and I didn't like to upset her because she sometimes let us sit inside when the weather was bad. I liked to visit her.

I was a little reluctant to show Old Ginger Paws this part of the Neighbourhood because I knew that he'd be cheeky and try to take more food than he needed. I usually only gave tours to cats who I could see were in genuine need of some food and shelter, like Sphinx. I walked into the garden of the third house and saw Old Ginger Paws eyes light up.

"This is a nice set up," he said.

"This is for one night only. These cats are in need and don't get themselves involved in the Neighbourhood fights unless they really have to. This land isn't up for territory. Do you understand?" I said.

If he or any of One Fang's gangs found themselves there, then there really *would* be a war, and quite rightly so. For some cats, this was their lifeline. I imagined that Patches had visited here once or twice, at least.

I made sure to walk Old Ginger Paws through the fence to the last garden. I wanted to make sure that if he thought that this territory was up for grabs, then I'd take him to the only house where I knew the humans weren't cat lovers.

The last house had a pond that contained koi. The fish always looked really tasty, and I'd seen many a cat get their whiskers wet when they were tempted to go fishing, myself included.

It wasn't my proudest moment. I saw the net over the top, and the humans greased the sloped sides. Of course, it wasn't immediately obvious that the sides were greased. I lifted the net up with one paw, put down my other paw and fell straight into the water. It was deeper than it looked as well. I went right under the water. The largest fish slapped me with its tail. I frantically swam to the edge and kept slipping in. One of the humans scooped me out, laughing, and he was right – I wasn't going to try that again.

I'd warned some cats because I knew that they wouldn't listen – every time they fell into the water! I thought if Old Ginger Paws was tempted, at least he'd fall into the water. It was just a shame that I mightn't be there to witness it for myself. I could've done with the laugh.

"What is it that you're so afraid of?" I asked.

"I've seen what he can do. I saw how he got you summoned to trial," he said.

"Go on, I want to hear who he knew to make that happen," I said.

Old Ginger Paws suddenly grew timid. He knew that telling me this tuna was leading him to the point of no return. If he told me this, then there was little to no chance of him ever making alliances with One Fang ever again. He had already said too much to me.

"I think you already know that he used Graphite to have you summoned. The Skittle Twins were always going to testify; they were too afraid of One Fang not to," Old Ginger Paws admitted.

"What was the real intention? Was he expecting a locked-in order?" I asked.

Old Ginger Paws nodded. It wasn't really a revelation. It seemed obvious that One Fang would try to do this. It wasn't that he was really scared of me; he just would've rather not had the thorn in his side as I wasn't giving up his land easily.

"He knew that Jet and Ebony would take you on the longest journey to the Burrow, so you'd lose your bearings. He had his whisperers set up so that you'd be attacked if you ended up in the other neighbourhood," Old Ginger Paws said.

"I must have really irritated him," I said.

"You annoy him. You're the only one who wasn't afraid of him. He hates that you're not intimidated by him. He hasn't fought properly with another cat in many years," Old Ginger Paws said.

I've to admit I was a little bit flattered that I annoyed One Fang so much. That was an achievement. It meant that I was enough of a distraction that he hadn't managed to take over Skinny's land straight away.

It also made perfect sense why Graphite turned so quickly on Sahara at the Stables. I thought it was strange that he turned against her, purely because she had offered me a place on the

Council without consulting him first. He was clever enough to bide his time and turn on her at her weakest moment. He felt betrayed and insulted that she had offered me the time to investigate Skinny's land. That made me smile. Even if Skinny's land went to One Fang, I'd made a dent in their egos. That felt good.

"One Fang is determined that he won't give Skinny's land back. He's going to make sure that you're summoned again to the Council. He wants you to be forever locked away," Old Ginger Paws said.

"What is it about Skinny's land that he wants it so much?" I asked, genuinely curious.

"It was his to begin with. It was a genuine kick to his ego to lose the land. He never forgave him," Old Ginger Paws said.

I could see that. It wasn't beyond reason that a cat would be frustrated that another cat had taken their land. However, the human clearly was more enamoured with Skinny Hind than he was with One Fang. That wasn't Skinny's fault. Sometimes, that happened. Besides, it wasn't beyond the realms of possibility that the human knew One Fang lived with other humans. He was only across the road.

"If Skinny returns home, One Fang is going to have to surrender the land. It's the Council's rules," I said.

"One Fang wants to cut a deal with him. He's got his cats searching for a human who might take him in," Old Ginger Paws said.

This was unheard of. The human was happy with Skinny, and Skinny was happy with the human. One Fang had to back off; that was all there was to it. One Fang could've easily given the land back; he had all of the other properties. He didn't need a perfect run.

"How does he intend to get that past the Council?" I asked.

The Council shouldn't have even considered that this was an acceptable change. It wasn't. Both the human and the cat would've been unhappy with this. Graphite needed to deter him from doing this.

Old Ginger Paws shrugged. I was sceptical. He'd told me a lot, but it didn't mean that any of it was true. I had to think a lot about what the gains would've been from this stalling. I didn't want Old Ginger Paws on my side: I never trusted him. Even without One Fang, I wouldn't have trusted him. I kept my cards close to my chest.

"What do you want from all of this?" I questioned.

"I honestly think you need to be aware that One Fang wants you incarcerated forever. I don't think that's fair – no cat should be unprepared for that. You haven't done anything to deserve that," Old Ginger Paws said.

It was difficult. Everything that he said was valid. I believed that One Fang wanted to have me off the streets to take Skinny's land and everything else that he wanted. It wasn't the first time that he'd cut his informants off for territory.

In the back of my mind, I also believed that One Fang sent Old Ginger Paws to deliver this message, in the promise that Old Ginger Paws would gain all of my territory.

"What does Graphite gain from all of this?" I asked.

"I don't know," Old Ginger Paws said.

The problem with Old Ginger Paws was that he was a good actor. I could quite easily accept that he didn't know, but if it was all part of the plan then he was doing a good job of convincing me.

*What do you gain from being here? Why me?*

"He's gone too far. If he's not stopped, he could do anything. He's already disbanded us because he doesn't know who he can trust. What will he do next?" Old Ginger Paws questioned.

It was ironic. If anything, One Fang had good right not to trust him. He'd found me immediately and told me everything, or that was how it seemed. I knew Old Ginger Paws found it difficult to confront me. I scared him because I'd defeated him too often.

Ultimately, I wasn't after creating an army of cats. I wanted a loyal circle of cats, who I knew I could trust. Cats were willing me to take One Fang on, and honestly, they had as much power as I did. It was becoming a chore. I needed to consult my watcher and whisperer, so I left Old Ginger Paws in the garden. I needed my team, and I needed them united.

Squirrel

# 18

## REALLY? HIM?

Curly Whiskers and Stripes were like family to me, but sometimes families don't get along. I needed the pair of them to put their differences aside because we needed to rely on each other. I headed to Stripes first. I knew that Curly would know where to find me.

As soon as I arrived, Skippy leapt down onto the first-floor roof. I shoved him hard against the wall. He fell back and bounced forward, sprinting as soon as he hit the ground. I wasn't keen on being taken by surprise. It was a low move that the shadiest of cats used. I always thought they did it because they were too scared to confront cats head-on.

"Stripes?" I called.

Stripes came down from the roof. She looked livid. I knew that she wasn't going to be happy when she saw that I was empty-handed, but I knew that she'd understand.

"I don't want to see any of those cats up here again," she said.

"We need to call a meeting with Curly straight away. I need you to step onto the street," I said.

I needn't have bothered. Curly was on the roof as soon as I finished my sentence. I didn't need to check; I knew that Shadows had visited him.

"What do you think?" I asked.

Curly shrugged. I knew he was sceptical of more than what Shadows had to say. I saw that he was weary of Stripes. He held his tongue, but I needed him to say what he was thinking. I needed to know whether or not they thought we should join forces.

"What?" Stripes hissed at Curly.

"You know as well as I do that you should've told us who informed you about Skinny. It shouldn't have been left until White Tip asked you. It's shady," Curly hissed back.

"Shady, who's shady? Don't think for a minute that you can call me that and not explain yourself. I should be able to rely on the pair of you without having to tell you everything. I'd never put you in harm's way without good reason. I had my reasons, I shouldn't have to justify myself. I thought we'd know each other for long enough," she hissed.

"It's sorted now, and we've discussed it. You need to trust each other. Otherwise, whatever decision we make, they'll use that against us," I reasoned.

Curly nodded his head. Stripes was far more stubborn. She hated being questioned by any cat, especially a cat who she thought should know her.

"Stripes?" I said. I needed her on board.

"Fine," she said.

"One Fang has stayed away from here. He hasn't been anywhere near, but it's obvious that he's surrounded by the Short Hair and some of the other cats," Curly said.

"Do we know which cats?" I asked.

Stripes shook her head. I knew that she wouldn't have seen any of the cats if One Fang headed back to Skinny's land.

"Did he turn around when he saw Old Ginger Paws – or any of them – execute the plan?" I asked.

Curly and Stripes shrugged their shoulders. They were at a loss – we all were. There was no knowing whether they were telling the truth. Only time would tell.

"Where are the Cat Council when you need them?" I hissed.

Autumn and Full Moon had to know that something was happening. Crinkles, Dolly, Jet, Ebony – the whole lot of them buried their heads. It made no sense. They should've been out there challenging Graphite, keeping him away from One Fang. There was no way that they didn't know about their friendship.

"They live on a different schedule," Curly said.

"There was a tonne of cats who headed over that way. There were lots of them," Stripes said. "I didn't know that they were from the Council or where they were heading."

"That was tuna that we needed to know," Curly hissed.

"The Council change their meeting spots," I explained. "She wasn't to know. Now might be the time when we get Sahara on our side. Graphite has ditched her. She'll be angry."

"Sahara?" Stripes asked.

"The Bengal," I said.

"It's too obvious. One Fang will know to watch you and any other cat heading over in that direction. He'll have that land surrounded," Curly said.

"Also, if Graphite was her closest friend, she'll still be in denial that he dropped her. She won't be easy to convince, nor will the others trust her," Stripes added.

"If we call Squirrel, he should be able to locate Autumn or Full Moon. Our best bet is to contact the Ragdoll," Curly suggested.

I'd never worked with Squirrel before, and at first, I thought Curly was low on sleep when he arrived. Squirrel was every bit as obvious as a dog. He was a terrible whisperer, especially with his big, red bushy tail. It dragged against everything. He might as well have worn a bell to announce his presence. I looked just to make sure that he didn't have a collar. His neck fur wasn't worn back any more than the rest of it.

"You trust our fate in him?" Stripes said.

"He's one of the best," Curly said.

Squirrel nodded his head a little too enthusiastically. His teeth overhung his bottom lip. He looked too clumsy to be inconspicuous.

"One Fang has no idea that Squirrel is a whisperer. He'll assume that he's here just to admire us, especially me. He'll think he's here to learn to hunt, which reminds me, you have your lesson tomorrow. Don't be late.

Remember to narrow your tail and feather paws, Squirrel. I need you to seek out Full Moon. He's an all-black cat with a white face. Whilst you're looking for him, you'll be approached by Autumn. She's reddish brown and will come from above. Her move is to land on you, and she'll pin your ear to the ground. You need to pass on the message that Graphite is rising," Curly said.

Squirrel nodded his head. His tail retracted into pure cartilage; I'd never seen anything like it. His steps were light enough that I thought he hadn't touched the floor. I was impressed.

"Will he make it to them?" Stripes said.

Squirrel was a fantastic decoy. He looked almost kitten like. He couldn't have been a year old. I was almost sure of it. It wasn't often that I was doubtful of Curly, or that I was wrong, but on that occasion, the answer to both of those questions was yes.

"There's no reason for him not to," Curly said.

"Will he be able to fight them though?" I asked.

Curly nodded his head, but I saw that he wasn't absolutely certain. It was a scary time waiting for the news, any news, good or bad. Even Curly had to do his best to remain calm. He combed his tail.

I nearly kissed the ground when Squirrel returned. I was pleased when he let his tail fan wide again. We knew that he was on his way.

"She said to meet her on Lock Jaw's land. It's the house in that direction with the two dogs' heads on the gate," Squirrel said.

I'm not going to lie about this; I was terrified. The last place I wanted to meet was on a dog's land, especially an unpredictable dog's land. It took all of my strength to pretend that I felt brave.

# 19

## LOCK JAW'S LAND

"Who is this Lock Jaw?" Stripes asked.

I wondered whether it was best to wait until he arrived or to just come out with it. It wasn't as if Curly knew either. I wasn't thrilled about having to meet him again. I waited until we were nearly there before I answered. Nerves got the best of me for a moment.

"He's a dog. He works with the Council," I said.

Stripes looked horrified. I noticed Curly was less surprised. He must have known who he was; of course he did. It was his business too.

"You seem awfully quiet," I said to Curly.

"What do you want me to say? You refuse to work with a lot of cats, but a dog doesn't seem to faze you," he said.

"Of course it fazes me. Do you think I want to be on a dog's property? I'd rather have nothing to do with him. You know that, but this was where Dolly said it had to be," I said.

I knew what the problem was. I'd refused to work with other cats, cats whom he deemed to be trustworthy, but I had high expectations. There were a lot of cats who just didn't have the markings of a trustworthy cat. I wasn't sure that I really wanted to be involve Dolly. I knew that there was far more to it than just this. It meant that I was in her debt for a long time; it meant choosing sides between which members of the

Council we believed in, and which we didn't. At that moment, it seemed straight forward there were some who wanted more power – Graphite and Sahara, and there were some who wanted to uphold democracy – Dolly and Crinkles. I still wasn't sure about the rest. An uprising can cause a tsunami if there are enough cats.

Why had Jet followed Graphite's instructions but didn't follow through on Sahara's orders? Something didn't add up. If Jet suspected a power play, she'd be doing her utmost to not be involved with it, even if she didn't want to be detected. If anything, she would've been creating obstacles.

"What made you trust Jet?" I asked.

Curly disapproved. I did too, if I was honest. I trusted Stripes, but how did we know that we could trust Jet? Just because she was a member of the Cat Council didn't mean that she was trustworthy. I mean Graphite hadn't proven himself, neither had the Skittle Twins. I hoped that there was far more to this than she was a member of the Council.

"I've known Jet for a long time," she said. "She's never done anything that I've been opposed to."

I wondered if Stripes really knew what she was getting into. She rarely spoke with any of the other cats. She liked to sit, unnoticed on her roof top. I wasn't sure she was worldly enough to make decisions about who she did and didn't trust.

Whatever my reservations, I had no right to question her judgement. She had higher standards than I did. I wanted to know what it was about Jet that made her trustworthy because I just couldn't see it. I thought she was indecisive. She kept herself quiet when the Council questioned Sahara. She should have been one of the first to question her, but she let Crinkles and Dolly do it instead.

"Time doesn't mean trust," Curly said bluntly.

He was right of course. A cat could turn at any moment. We all knew that. Land and food often came before loyalty. There were a lot of traitors.

"I never question your judgement, and you take in all of the waifs and strays," Stripes said.

That was completely true. There were few cats that Curly didn't trust. He usually took them in with open arms. To be fair to him he had never been betrayed so far. He was a good judge of character.

"He's rarely wrong though," I said. "What is it about Jet that you're wary of?"

"I think she rides with the tide. I think she acts upon something that another cat has told her, and then she fades back away. Was this her idea or was this someone else's?" Curly said. "You should've vetted her out before you got us involved."

I suppose my problem with Jet was that I didn't know enough about her. I didn't like venturing into the unknown. I liked to take my time to get to know cats before they got to know me. Of course, that wasn't always possible.

Perhaps I should've trusted Stripes' opinions as much as I trusted Curly's. It wasn't fair to place greater value in one than the other. If anything, the fact that Stripes trusted her, meant that we should have trusted Jet too.

"Skinny was missing, wasn't he? Nobody has seen him. She told me because she knew that I'd want to know. Have you ever questioned why you weren't informed?" Stripes said.

I could tell that Stripes had hit a raw nerve. Curly's tail began to fan out. Even so, none of what she said was actually wrong. They were all very valid points.

"Leave it now, both of you," I warned.

I didn't want the three of us arriving and causing a scene. I wanted as few cats as possible to know we were there, and it caused idle gossip from wagging tongues. It distracted instincts. Arguments were for other places, and at that moment, for other cats to have.

Lock Jaw's land was every bit as dog-like as I imagined it to be. The gate posts were each headed by a silver mastiff, wearing a spiked collar. Of course, the mastiff wasn't intimidating enough. I knew full well that he wasn't a *softie*.

The drive was paved with bricks and there was a huge dog bowl of water next to the front door, which only became apparent when you stepped around the massive car. I wondered how Lock Jaw moved around in that space. There was barely enough room for three cats.

"Hey, White Tip, I dare you to take a drink from his bowl," Curly laughed, and I was insulted. I wouldn't have shared rain water from the sky with a dog, let alone the same body of water.

"One Fang is keeping his distance at least," Stripes said.

For me, it wasn't so reassuring that he had decided to lock down on the property, making it a fortress. It meant that it was going to be near impossible to lure him away. We were probably going to have to fight on Skinny's land, which had us at an immediate disadvantage. None of us knew the land well enough to see the attack points or even the best hiding spots.

What felt reassuring was that at least the whisperers weren't coming down this far in the Neighbourhood. It felt as though we were more able to talk openly without the fear of being overheard. Perhaps there was a nugget of truth in what Old Ginger Paws said, after all.

Nervously, we sat and waited. The last thing that I wanted was for Lock Jaw to come bounding around the corner. The space was tight enough that we'd struggle if we needed to escape quickly. I hoped that Squirrel had got the message correct, and he hadn't been misinformed by Autumn.

"We're just around the back," Full Moon said.

So, we followed him around to the back of the house. The garden stretched back a long way. There were seats around a fire pit, with Dolly sat on one. It would've looked nice, had there not been a dog house in the corner. I wanted the meeting over with as soon as possible. That place gave me the creeps.

"Is he out here?" I asked, looking at the dog house.

"No, he sleeps indoors. He won't be out for hours now," Full Moon said.

That did little to ease my nerves. I suspected that his humans would allow him to chase off any unwanted visitors, especially cats.

"Please take a seat," Dolly said with a warm smile. "I'm glad that you came. The whole situation has developed into one huge mess. Did Autumn tell you that Graphite will be running for chair?"

I wasn't surprised. He wanted power from the beginning. It made perfect sense for him to be running for chair. The problem was which cats were going to support him?

"Who else is running?" I asked.

"So far, no one has come forward. It's a big job with a lot of responsibility," she said glumly.

"Would you rather he had the power and you all do as he said? He'll change everything. He'll pass rules and regulations, completely changing everything that the Council has worked for," I reasoned.

"Whoever runs, has the problem that if they lose, he will kick them out of the Council. He has a lot more followers than his opponent," she explained.

It seemed a strange situation that no one was running. If there was only one voice, that meant that Graphite might as well win the seat. He was probably already arranging his ceremonial parade as we spoke.

"When do you have to make a decision?" I asked.

The situation wasn't totally hopeless. One of the other cats might've been thinking that they would run, but hadn't announced it.

"By sunrise," she said.

# 20

# THE CLOCK WAS TICKING

D olly groomed her fur. She was strangely calm, as though she was sure of herself. I didn't care who was going to run, so long as it wasn't Graphite.

"It's going to be a horrible reign if Graphite gets tenure," Dolly said.

Full Moon turned to her. It wasn't often that Dolly spoke openly about her thoughts on other cats. She usually held her tongue. She was right though. I could see that Graphite was going to be a draconian ruler. He'd shown that by the way he'd been in the trial, and the way that he reprimanded Dolly at the Stables.

I knew that if Graphite ended up as the chair, that it didn't look good for Dolly. Graphite wasn't in favour of keeping her, not after she challenged him.

"Why don't you run?" Stripes asked.

Dolly was wise. She struck me as a good leader. She seemed to know some of the characters that she came up against, and she handled Sahara and Graphite well. It was a good suggestion from Stripes, but I knew that she wasn't going to run.

"Me?" Dolly confirmed. "No, I'm too old to run for chair, and I don't have enough followers. If they thought I was good enough, they would've asked me to run."

"Who would have asked?" I said.

"Crinkles, Jet, Ebony, one of them. They would've suggested that I run for chair," Dolly said. "The fact that they haven't means that they don't think I'm good enough."

I found it hard to accept hearing her talk that way. The way she spoke to Full Moon, and stood up to Sahara and Graphite made her an excellent leader. She was fair. The thought of Crinkles being a leader didn't appease me. There was more that he knew than he let on. There was a reason why none of them approached her. It was because they knew she was probably one of the best cats to be in chair. She was fair and stood up for what she believed in.

Dolly looked at Full Moon. He rose from guarding the gate, to sit by her. They stared into the sky, both of them looking at the moon. It was almost sombre.

Full Moon stood and walked around to the front of the house. There was no knowing what he was thinking. It was as though he was waiting for the bad news that Graphite or Crinkles had taken power.

I was suspicious of Crinkles. I wasn't sure whether or not he was at the trial, but he seemed to have a lot more power than he should've had. Why did he get to question Sahara? The Cat Council seemed to accept his word for not acting on One Fang's disrespect, a little too well. No one questioned whether it was the right decision to just allow One Fang to take over the land. It all seemed a little too easy, especially when the sole reason for us being there was to inform Sahara that he'd taken ownership of the land.

Sahara knew that One Fang was on the land, but she didn't care about it. She wasn't the only one, so why was she being punished for the general consensus? I wondered whether the reason the other members had been so keen to turn on her, was because they wanted another leader, Graphite. It made sense that none of the other cats wanted it.

I sent Curly and Stripes off to check up on Shadows, Skippy, and Old Ginger Paws. Curly and Stripes left immediately. It meant that I had time to think of my next move. I knew that One Fang was probably going to be surrounded, but the fewer there were, the easier it'd be.

I had no idea what to expect. I really didn't trust any of One Fang's gang, not even those who'd been betrayed. Every one of them could switch at any point, and I wasn't wholly convinced that One Fang would've disbanded them, unless they were trying to win Skinny's land for him.

Dolly jumped down from her seat. She looked like she was tracking something. She followed something scuttling across the stones. It was too dark to make anything out except that she pounced and then chewed it. I was a little shocked that a pedigree bothered with eating insects. They had prime meats in their bowl.

"I still like to make sure that I can hunt when I need to," she explained. "It's going to be a long night."

When Curly returned, Shadows stood behind him. I knew that she felt betrayed at the trial by One Fang, but it still took courage to be here. It pleased me that there was some truth in what they said, even if it was only her who showed up. I'd be lying if I said that I wasn't a little reluctant though. She'd worked for One Fang and she hadn't dropped him when she discovered that he was at the trial.

Stripes returned with the tabby, but there was no sign of Old Ginger Paws.

"He was gone. He's not anywhere that I can see," she said.

"It doesn't mean that he has gone back to them," Curly said.

I was disappointed. Every time I thought that Old Ginger Paws was going to come through with something and make the right decision, he let himself down. As far as I was concerned, he could go back to One Fang, and they'd probably take great delight in knowing I believed him for a small moment. I thought he'd turned his back on One Fang.

"He's a runner, White Tip. Runners don't stick around unless there are cats there to back them, literally all the time. You gave him no reassurance," Stripes said.

She might've been right, but it didn't mean that it stung any less. I should've thought about putting a cat with him for protection. It only took a light breeze to rustle a tree and he would've been terrified, especially without One Fang around.

Shadows was insistent that there was no way that Old Ginger Paws was going to be with One Fang. She said he'd released them. She appeared calm. I'm not sure I would've felt that way, if I'd been betrayed. Curly accepted this. He believed that we should trust her because it would've been difficult to leave a gang. There would've been all sorts of repercussions. Stripes sided with me. Once you were part of that gang, you were always a part of that gang.

"The lights were out on Skinny's land. Are his humans still living here?" Shadows asked.

"As far as I know. Thanks for the update," I said.

Dolly decided that she wanted news from the Council. She felt sure that Graphite was going to send for her, to have her removed. She sent Full Moon to find out whether any cats had come forward to run against him.

Curly and I went to check out Skinny's land. I needed to be close without raising the alarm. Fortunately, Curly had land that was right on the corner. The hedge wrapped around the corner, making it a perfect place to observe without being seen. Stripes watched out from above just to make sure. We had to make sure to walk across some of my properties, and then to cut across some of the other gardens, to get to Curly's land. It felt like an achievement just to arrive unscathed.

# 21

## HALF SEEN

Whilst we managed to see some of what was happening on Skinny's land, being close to the ground and looking through the hedge, made it difficult to really see what was happening. Skinny's house was definitely empty for the evening because the lights were off. The car was missing from the drive, but the human might have been out for the evening. There could have been any number of reasons for that. I wasn't about to jump to hasty conclusions.

"Who can you see?" I asked.

"Graphite is the only one I can see," Curly replied.

I found it hard to believe that One Fang and Graphite would be the only cats there. There had to be others. It was unlike One Fang to dispense of his cats. He was a cat who had multiple whisperers and multiple watchers. That told me that he wanted to know what was going on in the Neighbourhood. It said to me that he wanted power. Why would he just get rid of all of the cats that could lead him to some form of power?

Graphite also needed the backers. He needed the other cats to vote him in. Sure, he looked down on the common cats of the Neighbourhood, but he still needed the votes of cats who weren't in the Council.

"Just suppose that Old Ginger Paws went back to his human, does that mean that he is acting out what One Fang wanted?" Curly asked.

"I don't doubt that One Fang wanted this duplicity; it stalled time. I just can't believe that he wanted to lose his network of cats that he'd built up. This doesn't seem like him. This seems like the work of another cat," I replied.

Graphite had a real problem with common cats. He believed himself to be elite. One Fang was a Persian cat, so he was fine within his company. He was fine to speak with One Fang, and probably would have him voted into the Council. My problem was that I suspected One Fang wouldn't be the only cat who'd want to be on the Council. It'd work in his favour to have his whispers and his watchers elected; then, he'd know everything that was going on. I believed that he truly did want a friendship with cats like Old Ginger Paws. Ginger Paws looked big and intimidating, even though he wasn't. He'd already got my back up by approaching my land. That was enough for One Fang to want to associate with him.

Whilst favourable from a fighting perspective, my issue with cats being disbanded into the Neighbourhood was that they couldn't be trusted. They were used to a way of acting, disloyally. They were used to being sneaky and cunning to get what they wanted. Sneaking up on other cats, instead of fighting them head-on, was cowardly, in my opinion. It wasn't the way that I wanted to operate. I wanted cats to know that I was there. I wanted them to realise what they were up against.

I accepted that it took a lot of confidence for cats to be able to do that, but the unfair fighting was the behaviour of feral cats when they were hunted. We were civilised house cats. Cats had been domesticated and lived with humans for survival. We adapted our rules because we had to. If we'd continued being wild and attacking each other, we'd have lessened our numbers, possibly facing extinction.

Sure, the wild cats like lions, tigers, pumas, leopards, cheetahs, and lynxes had their freedom, and most cats would've loved that, but what were their survival rates? They had to sneak up on prey and sometimes each other for survival. We didn't have to do that. We were privileged, so we should've acted that way. I was all too happy to sneak up on food for hunting because it was necessary. When we had humans, we didn't need to do it to each other. That was how kittens did it.

I also wasn't about to welcome the cats with open paws because I didn't know their means of attaining land. How did One Fang distribute it? Did he allow for cats to take land, so long as they left his alone? Was One Fang really the cat who had so much territory, that he gave it away? Did they swarm to him because they felt that he could offer protection? I had no idea.

"I can see Brown Crown," Curly whispered.

Finally, there was a common house cat. I was surprised that Graphite was in his company. He was a common house cat like most of us. It was interesting that he allowed him to stick around. There had to be a good reason for why he was allowed to stay and some of the others weren't.

"White Tip, Skinny's human has returned. That's definitely his car," Curly said.

He'd barely finished the sentence, when I buried my face into the hedgerow. It wasn't the most comfortable places. The twigs scratched at my face and poked at my ears and cheeks, but it did provide a good view.

Skinny's human got out of his car and went over to the passenger side. He opened the door and carried out a plastic box. It was just like the one that my humans had for me. Then, he carried it to the front door. He never spoke to the cat, which I thought was strange because my humans would've reassured me. However, it was late, and he could've been sleeping. That was a possibility. This was hopeful!

The difficulty with the hedge and the distance meant that I had no way to look into the gaps of the box. There was no certainty that the cat was Skinny. It could've been any cat, even a new cat.

This was excellent news though, because it meant that One Fang and his gang would have to vacate the property. There was no chance that Skinny's human would stand for the other cats waiting around on the land, especially if they were going to fight Skinny. He'd used the hose on One Fang and me, so that had to say something. One Fang was going to be furious!

# 22

## NOW OR NEVER

It'd been ten days since Skinny had gone missing. It was a long time for any cat to be away from their land. Naturally, his land would've lost his scent. The scent faded within the first few days and coupled with One Fang's gang taking over, it made sense that it'd take a while for Skinny to feel at home again, if, of course, that *was* Skinny.

"How are you going to approach him?" Curly asked.

That was something that I hadn't really thought about. I knew that One Fang occupied all of the surrounding land, but if Old Ginger Paws was to be believed, he'd dismissed many of the cats watching it. That meant that it was easy to get to him, without many obstacles. It was possibly the perfect moment. However, a thought picked at my brain. The last thing I wanted was to find myself issued with a locked-in order by attacking a cat on pedigree land. I ruled out using the Skittle Twins land after what had happened the last time.

"I cannot go via the Skittle Twins property. What about the property to the left?" I asked.

"It's possible. It was where Shadows was operating, but now she's not working for him, you could try there," Curly said.

As far as I could see, it had to be the safest option. The land at the back of the property was the large field, which must have been one of the paths to the Stables. No one occupied the field because it belonged to all of the animals who wanted it. Who knew who lived there? It could've meant fighting foxes, badgers, or even horses. It was also too vast for a cat to ever take single occupancy of it. There were too many paths leading to it, that would make it too easy to invade it, and near impossible to police.

If I'm honest, I don't even think the Council would've stood a chance. They would've had to have been on the land all of the time. If a leash of foxes were there, then it would've been a nightmare. They had a lot of energy and they could've easily taken a number of cats all in one go. It might've been food for an evening, or maybe even longer.

I was sure that when One Fang took over the land, that even he only ventured so far before becoming overwhelmed set in.

Curly did his first checks to make sure that the coast was clear. The last thing I needed was for other cats to want to fight. I needed to save my energy. He stalked out, checking under cars and in the gardens. I knew that it might take some time for him to do his checks, so I wasn't expecting him to return. I sat with my back to the garden, looking through the hedgerow, when I felt a swipe at my tail. My head shot out. Curly laughed.

"You need to look out for those pesky cats," he laughed.

Pesky cats – he was lucky that I didn't swipe back! He was right though. I had to be on high alert at all times. They could come from any direction. They'd proven that many times.

I headed across the road and kept my head down. I tried my best to stick to the shadows. Sometimes, that was the problem with having black and white markings. The black was good camouflage, but the white, not so much.

The land was paved, with few plants. That made it much easier to creep across without stepping on twigs that might snap. I knew that One Fang and Graphite would be on high alert too. Any little sound could've tipped them off.

Skinny's human had gone into the back of the house. That made it easier to see what was happening, even in Shadow's garden. I managed to avoid the chippings around some of the plants. I was pleased to discover a gap in the fence, where the fence panel had come away a little. I saw four sets of paws. I could only guess who each belonged to. I knew three of the cats there – who was the other one?

"No I'm not watching from the front, that'll make it obvious that I'm working with you," Brown Crown said.

"I want to know what is happening out there!" Graphite hissed.

I imagined that Graphite was getting impatient. It meant that he was out of control. I liked that he felt worried. He was going to be frantic when he knew that Dolly was running against him.

"You have to sit back and wait for the results. Honestly, it means waiting a few hours," Brown Crown explained.

"I saw Autumn heading towards the Stables," a voice said. I recognised it, but I couldn't place which cat it was.

"Surely, she is not thinking of running again; nobody trusts her," Graphite said.

"There will still be some who will argue in her defence," the voice said.

"Well, I wouldn't trust her again, not after what she did. She was supposed to lock that Inspector White Tip away, and she granted him time to inspect the land! As if that wasn't enough, she offered him a place on the Council! Can you imagine? I put an end to it straight away. I knew that she had no idea about the Comrade Clause," Graphite said.

"I don't know what she thought she was doing; I imagine she was being playful," the voice said.

"Yes, well, it's tactics like that, that resulted in those non-breeds coming into the Council in the first place. I mean, do we really need the likes of Full Moon knowing our business?" he continued.

"He won't know for long, not when you're in power," the voice said.

"The two of you need to move into the shadows," One Fang warned. "The human doesn't like cats being on the land, unless it's Skinny Hind."

"Well, that cat is never coming back here, not after what I did to him, so the human will have to let you have it, especially if he wants the birds to be controlled," Graphite said.

It all made perfect sense! The reason why Skinny went away was that Graphite attacked him. Then, Jet – yes, that was it! The voice. It was Jet's.

# 23

## UNINTENTIONAL

My first instinct as a cat, when I saw injustice, was usually to attack. I couldn't help myself. If there was another cat on my territory, if I was hunting or was caught off guard, I had to attack. Reacting without questioning was what got me into that trouble in the first place. I wonder whether any of this trouble would've happened if I'd refused to take on the case.

One Fang had to know that about me. He had to know that I'd feel compelled to act. He wanted Skinny's land, so he'd agreed to work with Graphite in order to obtain it. He wasn't bothered if Skinny was needlessly or unjustly attacked, so long as he won the land. He would've watched the land and told Graphite when was the best time to strike. He'd watched that land for years. The entire time that I'd lived in the Neighbourhood, he watched Skinny's land for hours and hours on end. He'd do very little else.

When Graphite suggested that he'd attack Skinny, One Fang probably rubbed his paws together with glee. Finally, the plan was going ahead. He would have possession of Skinny's land.

It took little thought to think about Graphite had done it. He probably used the Skittle Twins property – or possibly Shadow's land – to gain access because that was only next door.

Then, that didn't make sense. One Fang had dropped Shadows. Since Graphite knew he'd attacked Skinny, it would've made her privy to the tuna. It would've been stupid to let her go. She would've known too much!

Graphite had to have used the Skittle Twins' land to gain access to Skinny's land. Skinny didn't venture out much into the Neighbourhood. He was quite happy with his human-land. It made sense; it was a fantastic bit of land. It looked like his presence was enough to keep bird numbers low, but he didn't bother hunting them because there were too many of them for him to have done that. The Skittle Twins would've never have questioned why Graphite needed the land because they were runners. They probably would've offered that he used it, so long as he didn't attack them.

That also made sense because the Skittle Twins were too scared to venture past the boundaries of their land. They also gave their land away to every cat that they came across. They stayed close to their land at all times. The only time they went beyond the boundary was when the Council held a trial. The only way they would feel brave enough to leave their boundary, would've been if One Fang had offered to provide guards to protect them as they went to the trial. Sahara might've known that they gave their land away freely, and because they were pedigree, other cats might not have questioned whether or not they were actual members. That made it possible to treat the case as treason. Of course, Graphite would've known that none of that was true, so it would've persuaded Sahara that they were members of the Council. No cats would've questioned the chair.

It took a while, but it was worth waiting until Skinny's human had switched the light off before I showed my presence. I knew that Jet and Graphite, at least, would have to leave the land because they were pedigrees. Their humans would be checking up on them and if they were missing for too long, they lost their privileges to go out around the Neighbourhood, at least for a few days. It didn't look good for a cat running for chair if they were unable to walk around the Neighbourhood. I suspected that One Fang would soon be leaving, but he had to make sure that Brown Crown went first. He didn't trust him not to steal the land. When he left, One Fang made one final check around the premises. He walked along the fence, sniffing and looking to make sure that no one was there. I made sure that I stood right in the light.

"White Tip!" he hissed.

To be honest, I would've rather have had the fight on Shadows' land, because there was less to be injured by, but I knew that One Fang couldn't scale the fence. He was much older than me. I was still able to jump on to the fence. I wasn't subtle, but that didn't matter too much. Skinny's human had been gone a while; I was willing to take a risk that we weren't going to be kicked off the land.

I made sure that I landed close to his feet. I wasn't about to use him as my landing spot. I wanted to make the ground shake when I landed. One Fang's eyes grew wide. His tail began to fan out. He was terrified. Of course he was. The light might have been dimmed, but I could smell it on him. He was used to using his one fang on his opponents. He needed to think fast.

We began to circle round. It was enough for some cats to make them run because both became more intimidated about making a move. It was like allowing the build-up to overcome you. I launched forward and hissed in his face. I expected One Fang to hiss back at me. Instead, he did the last thing that I would have ever expected him to do – he sprinted.

I watched him run from the garden. I was impressed that I didn't have to fight. That rarely happened. I usually had two or three scratches, at least, from a small scrap that I'd had, or from Curly thinking it was funny to take a swipe at me. The fact that I came away without a mark, I was impressed.

The problem with running was that it often meant that the runner wasn't concentrating on anything else, but escaping. One Fang was so set on being off Skinny's land; that he never looked where he was going. Skinny's human was so good at tidying the garden and looking after the property, that it would've been reasonable enough to assume that everything was in its normal place. Except on that day, he'd left the hose trailing across the ground. One Fang tripped on it and headed face-first into the wall.

One Fang yowled out in pain. I knew straight away what had happened. He was yowling for far more than being a little hurt.

I walked over to him. I saw that he was devastated, but then One Fang squeezed through the gate and ran home. I never expected that to happen. I stood on the parts of his tooth. It was pretty sharp, no wonder it hurt. He lost the biggest part of his identity.

It was strange. I expected that when I won the land back for Skinny Hind that it'd feel cathartic, but it didn't. It felt disappointing, probably because I didn't actually do anything – it was luck. The only thing that I felt good about was that when Skinny returned – if he returned – then he didn't have to fight for his land back.

I headed straight for Curly Whiskers. I crossed the road and as I went to pass the car, I felt the familiar swipe at my legs.

"Sorry," he said, "I didn't think it was you because you're back so soon."

His apology would've meant more if he wasn't laughing when he said it. He'd managed to get me twice in one night. I knew where I stood with Curly though, which was more than what I could say about One Fang.

He'd lied about me before, so I was cautious. Now, every cat knew that he was working with Graphite. It made it easier for him to bring an issue before the Council.

Besides, if Graphite won, it meant that I'd probably be facing another locked-in order. I could have kicked myself. The worst thing, of course, was that there was no way I could've stopped that. I had no idea that One Fang was going to run.

"One Fang will have to go to the vets. There's no way that his humans won't take him when he's broken a tooth," Curly tried to reassure me.

Curly wasn't surprised that he was a runner. He expected him to do just that because I'd faced him honestly and fairly. I'd taken away his signature move.

It wasn't often that Stripes came down to ground level, but of course, even she was curious when she saw that One Fang fled from Skinny's land across the street.

"There's no way that he'll be able to bring about a trial in time. He's not a Council cat, so Graphite won't have any control to have you locked-in. He's fallen out with Sahara, so no one will believe that One Fang is a member," Stripes said.

Stripes turned to leave, but I stopped her. She needed to hear it from me that she'd been betrayed. I couldn't have forgiven myself knowing that I had known who'd attacked Skinny and then not relay that tuna back to her.

"Stripes, Graphite was the one who got Skinny sent away," I said.

Stripes normally acted so aloof that it was near impossible to see her show emotion. She came across as cold a lot of the time. When she reacted to the news, she seemed to become so vulnerable; it was almost kitten like. I knew that she'd seen things. She hadn't been protected from the Neighbourhood, but her emotions were sometimes so raw, they didn't always appear cat-like.

She stood frozen; her breath silent, it was like she wasn't breathing. I'd never seen anything like it before. Then, anger crossed her face. She gnashed her teeth. Her fur stood on end. I was frightened, but there was more. I had to fight through the pain.

"Jet knew it was him," I said.

Sometimes, it was difficult to have honest conversations. Cats didn't react the way that either you wanted to or expected them to. Not all cats liked to receive the truth. At that moment, I wasn't sure that Stripes appreciated knowing that Jet had broken her trust.

Stripes just stared into the abyss and never uttered a word. It became uncomfortable. Her nostrils quivered. That was the only way that I knew she was actually still alive.

"Stripes?" I asked.

"She came up to my roof and she told me, because she thought I should know, that Skinny was missing. Was he even missing for three days?" she asked.

I shrugged. It didn't really matter whether Skinny was missing for one day or three. The only way we were ever going to know that for sure was if we asked Skinny himself. I was hopeful, but there was no certainty that he was alive. Then, I looked at Stripes, and I knew that this meant the world to her. She needed to know whether Jet had lied about everything, or whether she had told some grain of truth.

"Stripes, she let you down. She knew that Graphite had done that to Skinny and she pretended as though she didn't. She's a rat," Curly hissed.

Stripes looked wounded. There was only so much that she could take. She'd already taken her quota of bad news for the day. I realised that this was why she rarely set foot on the ground. She was afraid of being hurt. She trusted so few cats, so when she took the chance on a new cat, they let her down.

"She could have had any of us fooled," I said.

"She didn't though," Stripes wept. "Curly knew, you knew. You tried to warn me, but I wouldn't listen."

The reason I worked with Curly and Stripes was that they were loyal. When they got things wrong, they felt guilty. I liked that they could admit that. It took a lot of courage. Stripes left to go back up to her roof; she needed time away to think about everything. Besides, I wanted to make sure that Curly wasn't thinking about dropping Stripes anymore. That wasn't good for us, especially not at that moment.

If I thought things had gone wrong, I had no idea how bad they could be.

# 24
## GOODBYES

The air seemed still. That should have been the first warning sign. It was unusual for the whole Neighbourhood to be silent. There was always something to be heard – a cat crawling from under a fence, a cat fight or even the sound of something hunting. To not hear anything was strange.

As Curly and I walked over to Lock Jaw's land, we should've noticed the tension. We entered through the front gate onto the drive and walked around the path to the back garden. Full Moon was there to greet us. He nodded. Dolly sat looking into the abyss. She was upset about something. They were alone. Where had Shadows and Skippy gone?

"Sahara is back in the running," Dolly admitted.

If I had been stood closer, I think I might have seen actual tears in her eyes. She couldn't even look at us as she spoke. Her head was bowed.

I couldn't believe that Sahara had backing from any of the other cats. It didn't seem to make sense. They'd removed her power, but supported her running. Then, I realised that this was all a part of the plan. None of them were going to vote for her, because they felt as though she couldn't be trusted. They were all going to back Graphite!

"Where did Shadows go?" I asked.

Dolly's head shot up, but there really wasn't time to wallow. She looked around the garden as if shocked that we were the only ones there. Then, when she found no answers, she looked at the moon.

"She left a while back," Full Moon replied.

Full Moon never moved from his position. He sat almost statue-like, looking at the entrance to the garden. His tail was tucked around his legs. The floor was cold and uncomfortable, but he didn't seem to notice. I could tell by his pose that he never thought to ask her as she left.

I wondered whether Shadows was coming back. The way he sat, made me think that maybe she was on her way to deliver a message, but there was no work for her to do. She was redundant. The only place that Shadows could've been heading was home, wherever that was.

"Will she be coming back?" Curly asked.

"I'm not her keeper!" he snapped.

Curly had never known Full Moon to react. Curly sat back. Only I had seen Full Moon defeat Patches. I understood his anger. I knew that he'd lose some of his power; Graphite would want him gone too. He didn't care for cats who weren't pedigree. It was a matter of pride – I understood that. However, when he knew what the future held, it made no sense for him to remain angry. He needed to work with us.

I walked over to sit in front of Dolly. I needed to confess to her what happened with One Fang.

"Inspector White Tip?" she asked.

"I need you to know that when One Fang tells you I broke his tooth, I didn't," I replied.

Dolly looked confused. She wasn't expecting me to say that. She wanted to know more about the story, but I wasn't going to tell her straight away. She looked at Full Moon, then back to me.

"I trust you Inspector White Tip," She said. "You have shown me no reason not to."

147

Unsure of when she was going to snap, I felt nervous as I told her. She'd already been let down by the rest of the Council.

"I'm sad to say that I'm not surprised," Dolly said.

Dolly kept herself quiet. I wanted to know what Jet has done to make herself so sketchy in Dolly's eyes. Dolly was secretive though. She wasn't one to be gossiping.

Full Moon calmed himself down. He came and sat by us. It was rare that he offered advice; it was no surprise that he still didn't.

I wasn't expecting any guests. When Autumn dropped down onto the ground in front of us, I nearly jumped out of my skin. She seemed to be able to act with the same discretion as Squirrel could. I wondered if they were related.

There was something about Autumn that I found relatable. She had a lot of respect for Dolly, enough that she knew to come when she heard the news that Sahara was running. She knew too, that Graphite was going to kick her out of the Council.

"I wish it could have been another way," Autumn whispered.

Dolly smiled. She was good friends with Autumn. Dolly knew that she could no longer talk with her. Autumn was the watcher for the Council. It seemed they'd already sacked Full Moon from his role.

Autumn vanished, as quickly as she arrived. I assumed that she was on official business. Being seen with Dolly was no longer an option. It was a sad sign of things to come. Before she left, she said, "Inspector White Tip, you will want to disappear for a while. Graphite knows about One Fang's tooth."

# 25

## A NEW CHAIR

I woke with a sore head. I didn't end up going home until the early hours, just before sunrise. The Duchess always had a rule that if I wasn't back before she went up to bed, then I had to stay outside. It allowed me to deal with any problems I needed to sort out. It didn't happen often, but when it did, it helped. The Male One usually came out looking for me, which meant that I had to hide. Sometimes, if I was close to my land, there wasn't too much damage control. But if I wasn't, I found myself in some big trouble. Usually, it meant having a much bigger fight than I intended because I was on another cat's land. It didn't always make me too angry. It was how I ended up with my eight o'clock cuddles.

I slept in the garden, and woke to the sound of wood pigeons. I hadn't caught one of them recently, and they were starting to get a little over-confident. They left their markings all over the drive and the cars. The problem was that they were too high. There was no roof for me to jump from. My house next door had a conservatory, but the roof sloped. I didn't fancy my chances on the roof. I once stood on the guttering, and it started to come away. I sat against the wall.

Every few minutes, one swooped over, onto the fence; grabbed a few berries, and then back again. They all looked into the trees; then they flew back. Not one of them looked

149

at the garden below. Each time, they became more daring, swooping lower and lower. I tiptoed over to the overgrown grass. When it swooped over, I pounced – breakfast.

I quickly went back into the grass. I didn't want the other birds to have to watch as I ate one of their buddies.

When the next one flew out, to check on their friend, I pounced again. I owed Stripes breakfast. I decided to take the scenic route. I didn't want more members of the Council coming after me. I knew I'd be okay. The next house was mine. Granted, it was a night house because there was a little terrier that liked to bark at me.

As soon as I landed, the little mutt was there growling at me. He kept telling me to keep away if I knew what was good for me. I landed on the floor and I put my catch down. The little mutt was only slightly bigger than the pigeon that I ate. I was still a little hungry. He gnashed his teeth at me, so I arched my back and hissed in his face. He soon whimpered and ran off inside. I picked Stripes' breakfast up and carried on my way.

Stripes was sat looking out, as usual. I wondered why she never bothered with the ground or her humans. The decking area had chairs with the largest, comfiest cushions I'd ever seen. Why would she want to sit on roof tiles instead of on a comfortable chair? I knew where I'd rather be.

I called her down to the lower roof. Her eyes lit up when she saw the wood pigeon. It'd been a while since I'd caught something large. Stripes was impressed. She'd seen them messing up the place and asked a few times why I hadn't bothered to catch one. I usually hunted when it was necessary, no matter where I was that day. I didn't usually go out of my way for anything specific.

"Old Ginger Paws hasn't been over to Skinny's land," she said. "He's just sat on his human's land."

"Skippy?" I asked.

"She's over there," Stripes said.

I had to squint, but when I knew where to look, I spotted her straight away. She was curled up, sleeping on the roof. Not many cats can climb to their roofs. Many watchers didn't have humans, so it was understandable that Skippy took advantage of this and found refuge on a roof.

"Do you think we should believe them?" I asked.

If there was going to be any scepticism, it was going to be the strongest from her. I knew that Curly was a little more forgiving. I wanted someone who was more objective, judgmental even.

"I think they were once part of One Fang's gang," she said. "None of them have been near him since, and I've not seen him looking for them."

That was unusual. One Fang kept his cats close. They usually travelled in two's or more. They came almost as a pack. Fewer cats wanted to challenge them, especially alone. I suspected that Old Ginger Paws was feeling pretty rejected by now.

I almost felt sorry for Old Ginger Paws. There was no one for him to hang around with. I don't think One Fang ever worked on ensuring that his cats got along with each other. Old Ginger Paws kept away. He didn't want everyone knowing that he'd been dropped. He didn't want others to talk about him. He wasn't used to having to find new friends. He thought he'd found some, and then they fell out with him. There was no one to look out for him and no one to tell him where to go or not. It must've been lonely, but he made his choices when he joined One Fang.

I felt sorry for him. Any help I was going to give him was minimal. I didn't trust him, but I was going to help him.

I walked over to his land, I would've normally walked right under the gate, made my presence known. I didn't want him to run though, so I just popped my head in to check that I was invited. I offered him a bit of respect, even if he didn't offer it me. Old Ginger Paws nodded his head. I scrambled under the gate. He lay on his side, showing his belly to the world. It was good that he trusted me, but he seemed to have a lot of faith. It could've been anyone that walked in there. He was on his own land. He should've been able to sit however he wanted to. I just thought he would've been warier given the circumstances.

I sat down near him. I wasn't about to lie on my side, showing that I trusted him. I was still a little cautious. Besides, I wasn't entirely sure that he hadn't just given up.

"Have you heard anything from him?" I asked.

"Not since he told me to go. He told all of us to go," Old Ginger Paws replied glumly.

I saw that he was going to get upset if I kept asking him questions about One Fang. He trusted him, and he was hurt that One Fang didn't trust him. It was painful. I had to ask questions, but not about him.

"How about Graphite?" I asked.

Old Ginger Paws sat up. His eyes narrowed and his lips curled. His tail swished this way and that. I knew that he blamed Graphite for everything that had happened with One Fang.

"No, and it wouldn't be a bad thing if I never heard from him again," he hissed.

I decided to take my chance and tell him that Graphite was running for chair. He was going to find out soon anyway. It was better that he heard it from me rather than on the streets. That would've been a shock for him. I explained what happened with One Fang. If the pair of them ever joined forces again, he could hear the story from him. I'm sure One Fang would have a different version of what happened, but whilst Old Ginger Paws was there, I thought it was worth telling him my account.

Old Ginger Paws seemed to understand. I saw that he still had the instincts to be defensive for One Fang. He seemed angry. His tail stood on end. He looked at my face and realised that he no longer had to fight for One Fang and calmed down.

"Did you know that Graphite was the one who attacked Skinny?" I asked.

He lifted his head, looked me in the eye, and I knew that he did. I was livid. He should've told me! He knew that we were searching for Skinny. As soon as One Fang dropped him, Old Ginger Paws should've admitted that tuna straight away. He'd let me down again!

"Who else knew?" I hissed.

"White Tip, I only guessed. I was never told or saw Graphite. I don't know," he said.

I saw that Old Ginger Paws was starting to get nervous. He tucked his feet under him and made himself as small as possible. I didn't want him to run. I wasn't really in the mood to chase him. I hadn't had much sleep, so I needed to conserve my energy – I knew that Graphite was out looking for me.

"Who has he got over there?" I hissed.

"I...d...don't know." Old Ginger Paws said.

I ran from his land before he could run himself. I needed to find Curly quickly. If we were going to help any of One Fang's old gang, they needed to start helping us.

# 26

## BACKGROUND STORIES

S tripes woke Skippy and demanded that she met me on the ground. For a cat that'd just been woken up, she had a surprising amount of energy. She met me on the ground within seconds.

"You need to tell me who Graphite and One Fang are with," I said.

At least she was smart enough to know not to question whether she should or not. At that point, I would've handed the lot of them into the Council to make them Graphite's problem. He could have the whole lot of them on a locked-in order.

Skippy jumped back up. She watched for some time, and then she joined us back on the ground. I hoped that she knew some of their names or at the least gave good descriptions so that we knew who she was talking about.

"I don't know everyone, just Brown Crown, One Fang and Graphite. I've no idea who the Cornish-Rex is," she said.

"When he dismissed you, who did it? Was it One Fang or Graphite?" I asked.

"One Fang said very little. Graphite thanked us for our service, but he said we needed to leave. We wouldn't be needed for anything from now on, we couldn't be trusted. We had come far enough," Skippy said it through gritted teeth.

"Where was One Fang whilst he said that?" I questioned.

One Fang usually acted much smoother than that. Even I knew that. He told little lies that started to build as time went on. It was only after cats had heard lots of the lies, that they became hurt and felt betrayed.

"He just sat at the side with his head bowed, saying nothing," she said bitterly.

I imagined that would've been humiliating. There was no way that I would've gone back to him after he allowed Graphite to speak to me like that.

"Why did Brown Crown get to stay?" I asked.

Skippy had no idea. She was bitter about the whole thing. It was interesting that One Fang was happy to have them seek out tuna, but told them nothing at all. Brown Crown had to know something that the others didn't. There was no way that Graphite would've let him stick around. He was a common cat.

"Who are the other watchers that he has?" I asked.

Skippy was a better informant than Old Ginger Paws. She felt bitter, not sad. She wanted revenge on One Fang. It was the perfect time to ask her because she was no longer in a state of shock. She was on her own in the Neighbourhood. She needed the support of cats, she told us.

I'd seen Two Prints; he was unusual. His face was one-half ginger and one-half tortoiseshell. The rest of him was tortoiseshell. He kept to the tree that was outside One Fang's land. I should've known that he was working for One Fang. He rarely stepped onto the ground, so I didn't really notice him.

Two Prints probably tipped One Fang off that I was on Skinny's land. He didn't have the best view of everything. The tree wasn't very tall. He hadn't come to me because he never actually wanted to work for One Fang. Skippy informed me that One Fang made sure he approached him whenever he was on the ground.

It would've been so irritating to have had him pestering him all of the time. I'm sure that he only agreed to work with him, so that he'd stop pestering him. He wouldn't have given him a lot of tuna. One Fang had to approach him. He only had to see or spot one thing to keep him happy. He was probably grateful when Graphite sacked him.

I'd never seen Smudge. I got the impression from what Skippy said that she was shy. Smudge agreed to work with One Fang because she was intimidated by him. Just like Two Prints, she wanted to be left alone. Skippy told me that she had longed to retire to be a house cat, and when Graphite sacked her, her dream came true.

As we walked over to my eight o'clock cuddles, Stripes wanted to know why I didn't want to work with her. It was simple really. She wasn't loyal. She gave me that tuna without knowing what I might do to One Fang. Stripes surprised me because she thought that I was harsh. I wasn't sure that I wanted Skippy working for me. She gave me tuna that I needed, which I was grateful for, but I wasn't going to make a decision to work with her just yet.

Curly was already there. He'd brought Shadows. I wasn't so keen on her knowing where my land was, or thinking that it was okay for her to be there. I wanted to have some privacy. I didn't have anywhere else that I could host a meeting.

Shadows was bitter too. I already knew that from the trial. She had no idea that he was going to be there. If he trusted her, he would've told her. She felt cheated. I wanted to know why she forgave him.

"Humans don't tend to like black cats," she said.

One Fang gave Shadows some land. The humans fed her. They were quite impressed to have her around, but One Fang never let her forget it. He held it over her as though she owed him a favour forever. She felt forever in his debt. I expected that the humans probably liked having Shadows around and she no longer owed him anything.

"Graphite told me that I wasn't to go back," she wept.

There was more to Shadows than this one story. I knew that. It took a while for her to admit that humans left her in a glass box when she was a kitten. It took other humans to find her and take her to a rescue centre. She thought that she'd be picked. The centre lost money and then the humans set the cats free. Shadows had to find herself a new home. She didn't have survival skills because she was only a kitten when she was taken to the rescue centre.

I was shocked to discover that One Fang took it upon himself to protect her from other cats in the Neighbourhood. She worked hard for him. She felt like she owed him for her new life. That was why she never walked away from being a whisperer!

I walked Shadows through the Neighbourhood. We stopped at a lamp post. She was confused, until I asked her to look up. There, stuck to the lamp post, was Shadows' face. The humans were looking for her. She needed to know that she could return to her land. The humans had chosen her. It was no longer One Fang's land to snatch it back.

"You don't allow him or any other cats on your land. You need to make sure that you keep them off the land," I warned.

One Fang might have ensured that Shadows was protected from other cats, but she still needed to know how to fight. I agreed to mentor her. She needed to know how to stand up to all of the cats who Graphite walked through her land. He'd succeeded before in intimidating her, by relying on her weakness. I wanted to ensure that he didn't do that again. That went against everything that One Fang had set up for her.

# 27

## BRUTALLY HONEST

When Autumn stepped onto my land, my heart was filled with dread. I thought she might be there to tell me that I'd been summoned to the Cat Council to receive a locked-in order. From the incline, I thought we were heading towards the Burrows.

We turned left when we reached the path. I was sure that we were going in the wrong direction, but I wasn't about to question Autumn. She was the main informant to the Council; she knew the direction. It wasn't for me to question.

We walked much deeper into the path than I knew. The ground changed from stone to mud. Wherever we were going, it was definitely somewhere that I'd never been before. The trees and the undergrowth made me think that we were going deep into the woods. We turned off the path, to the left, to tread through the mulch. My paws were getting filthy.

Suddenly, we found ourselves walking through a farm. There were hay bales on both sides and a strong smell of manure. I assumed horses lived here. There were large machines that I'd never seen before. I was relieved that the engines were switched off. We climbed in between the gate and onto a stone path again.

When we came to a burrow, I became nervous. It looked so small that I wasn't sure I was going to fit. How did the

158

Council fit into there? Autumn warned me to keep my head low. We seemed to walk for a long time, and I was almost sure that the tunnel was becoming narrower.

Autumn lifted a grid. We had to scramble up into the space. I was pleased that we'd reached civilisation. I took a deep breath. I knew the space – it was the Stables.

Sahara closed the grid.

"Thank you, Autumn," she said.

Sahara led me towards the stables where Patches had been. For a moment, I thought I was being incarcerated until we took a seat in her office. There were two chairs sat on either side of the desk. It had to belong to her humans. Why would a cat have a space like that, just for themselves? She sat watching me. I hoped that she wasn't expecting me to speak first.

"I owe you an apology," she said after an uncomfortable silence. "I should've sent for One Fang earlier. I've been naïve and foolish."

It was well-deserved, but I wasn't expecting it. It bowled me over how humble she was being. I knew that she was foolish, naïve, and vain.

Sahara wanted me to be honest with her, but I don't think she contemplated quite how straight forward I'd be. I told her that she needed not to be so easily offended. I wasn't there to massage her ego. If she wanted my advice, she needed to know that I'd be blunt.

"I don't think that you will win. It isn't testimony to your character. You've been naïve in trusting Graphite and ignorant about what he was doing. He fed you compliments, and you never questioned any of that. The whole time he was working on the way to get himself into power," I stated.

Sahara nodded her head. She wasn't used to cats being so honest with her and looked defeated. She didn't want to give up her power but wanted to fight for it.

Cats didn't trust her. Crinkles had made sure of that when he questioned her. Graphite had built this up over a long period of time with others' help. It was a difficult truth to swallow. She'd been betrayed by the cat that she believed she could trust. However, she'd sometimes acted without consulting him and enjoyed watching his shock. Sometimes, she wanted to show him that she held the power. She provoked Graphite. She'd betrayed his trust as much as she had betrayed his.

It was a challenge to be empathetic with her. I'd seen her intimidate Dolly, and she was supposed to be a friend. She was shocked when Dolly stood up to her. Dolly knew more than her. She knew when Sahara was wrong. When she went too far, Sahara was shocked that Dolly put her back into her place. Sahara had ultimately pushed Dolly too far.

"I saw what happened with One Fang," Sahara said.

I waited for Sahara to use that tuna in some way. I expected that she'd use this as a bargaining tool to get me to help her, but she didn't. Bribery wasn't her style, which restored some of my faith. The members of the Cat Council were supposed to be the good ones, upholding the rules and making sure the Neighbourhood served us all.

"There will be consequences for this. I know that Graphite will seek revenge somehow, so if you need to take refuge here, then you can at any point," she said.

She went to explain that she thought Graphite would sack Dolly and Full Moon as soon as he stepped into power. I knew that much, and so did they. Sahara wanted them to stay away from the Council for some time.

"I've looked over some rules, and now I know that unless they attend the meeting, he cannot get rid of them officially," she said.

It was good to know that she consulted the rules now and again, when it suited her. I told her that I knew the Skittle Twins weren't members, as did Graphite and probably most of the Council. Sahara sat up straight up and adjusted her paws. Her face stayed straight.

"How did I not know this?" she asked.

"I suspect it's because you trusted them all. They should've been making sure that they upheld your trust – the ones who knew. Graphite knew that you trusted him and would never question what he said. Then, when it came from you that they were, even though you'd never noticed them at meetings before, you didn't want to look foolish. You kept up the charade. The ones, who didn't know, were none the wiser. Those who did know didn't challenge your power. They knew that cats from all over the Neighbourhood were there," I said.

Sahara knew that Graphite had betrayed her. He'd made her look like an incompetent fool. By creating a situation where she wouldn't know the answer – but he would – she wouldn't want to look as though she was ignorant and had never noticed the Skittle Twins. It was clever.

I had to hand it to Graphite; whether these creations came from him or another, they were well thought out. There was no doubt that he was intelligent. He knew how to make cats trust him. If another cat had tried to convince the Council to drop Sahara, then they'd have failed. The Council would have their membership revoked. Yet, it was genius to convince Crinkles and the rest of the Council that Sahara was involved in a power play.

Graphite was also an excellent strategist. Dolly had called a meeting for the pair of them. I was sure that she wanted the Council to know about both of their behaviours. He'd intimidated her, just as much as Sahara had, but by sitting away from her, he could detach himself.

Sahara listened. When I explained how Graphite had done it all, something seemed to switch in her. By stepping out of the victim role, she was ready to fight back because she was angry.

Anger could sometimes be a useful emotion. It was better than sadness. Many times, I'd seen anger propel a cat into action. For example, with that car, Patches sent that message out loud and clear. But most cats didn't send their messages to humans.

It would've been useful in this situation, so long as Sahara understood that she could only act for her position as chair. Anything else that she wanted to do, revenge or otherwise, was too far. Whenever cats went beyond what they wanted to achieve from their anger, they always ended up where they didn't want to be. I believed that Sahara had been through a lot. She didn't need to be back there.

I was curious to know why Autumn had still acted as her messenger, despite working for Graphite. It seemed a conflict of interests. Sahara explained that Autumn was a whisperer and a watcher for the Council. She had to be an informant to both until a chair was chosen.

As much as it hurt Sahara, I thought it best that she let Graphite win. I saw it as an opportunity for the rest of the Neighbourhood – especially the Cat Council – to see whether or not he could be a good leader. I suspected not, but that was for them to decide. Everything about what Sahara was running for looked as though she was seeking revenge. It wasn't a competition, and it shouldn't have been. If she was going to hold up the integrity of the Council, she had to allow Graphite to run. The decision hurt her, but there was little time to convince the rest of the cats that she was the better leader.

# 28

## GRAPHITE FOR COUNCIL

Knowing another way to the Neighbourhood had its benefits. I didn't want to be seen by any of Graphite's cats if I could help it. There was less chance of being seen this way. As I got to the top, it was easy to see where I'd gone wrong the last time. The last time I turned left, when my Neighbourhood was right.

One Fang had done a good job of recruiting cats from the other neighbourhood. How had he done it? He was a terrible fighter. He'd have to win over their gangs of cats, and I was intrigued.

I considered going back, but wanted to know what it was like in this Neighbourhood. Everything was much easier to see when it was light. I made sure to walk a bit further, not wanting to land in the creature's garden again.

Though I hesitated in my choice to stay in this Neighbourhood because there seemed to be a lot of dogs, fortunately, the Jack Russell was behind gates. They could be lively and good at biting. He tried to tell me not to go onto his land, but I wasn't going to anyway. I was looking for cats. I wanted to find where that little gang of four were. I looked under cars and behind bushes, but there were no cats there. *Where was that gang?*

As I walked to the end of the street, I knew I recognised where the road led to. It was the Neighbourhood. I was quite impressed with myself. I knew that I had to walk fast though; the land wasn't my land.

I felt a pair of eyes on me. They burned through my fur so much I turned around. But no one was there. I carried on, looked up, and couldn't see any watchers. There were no trees on that side, so I only had to look at the rooftops. I crouched down and saw there were two sets of eyes on me.

"Inspector White Tip!" Patches hissed.

It was the first time that I ever thought about running from a cat – Patches was vicious. I was sure that he wanted to get me back for what happened on Dolly's land. I reminded myself that I wasn't a runner. I didn't want that reputation. When there was a tale that a cat was a runner, suddenly a full library opened about them. They seemed to attract more fights, especially if they had a lot of land. I didn't have a lot, but I had enough to feel the loss and stuck around.

"Patches, are you going to come out?" I asked. "Talk in the open?"

I suspected that Patches was annoyed that he couldn't sneak up on me. I'd ruined his plan. Big deal! Patches didn't care about that. He fought anyone, whether they saw him or not.

Patches told me that I needed to crouch low. He wasn't prepared to talk to me out in the open. It was smart really. I understood that he didn't trust many cats either. I crawled underneath. For a small cat, he seemed to take up a lot of space. I found myself curling up as small as I could go.

"The Short Hair sent me away. Apparently, the land was never meant for me. I'd misunderstood," Patches said with a grunt.

Was he cross because I was right? I'd warned him that One Fang was never going to give up the land. Perhaps he thought that he'd be the exception. That wasn't like him.

"I'm supposed to bring you to Graphite, but I'm going to let you pass," Patches admitted.

I was grateful. That had to mean that Graphite wanted to place a locked-in order on me. Although, as far as I knew, he wasn't the chair yet. He couldn't do that until he was, and it had to be in the presence of four members of the Cat Council.

"Why are you working for him after he did that?" I asked.

"He's the new chair of the Council. No one is allowed to refuse to work for them," Patches said. "He's just brought that rule in."

For them? I didn't like the sound of those words. I wasn't gone for long, maybe a couple of hours, and he was already the chair of the Council. Few chairs brought in their new rules immediately. That was a bad sign. Patches told me Sahara had already backed down before my paws landed in the Neighbourhood. I expected her to act on my advice; I didn't realise that she was going to do it so suddenly. Without anyone to oppose, it made sense to make him the chair.

I liked the way Patches refused to work for Graphite properly. He had principles and was playing him at his own game, pretending to do what he was told, but was doing what he liked. Patches didn't care who saw him though. He knew that the only place he could be sent to was The Stables and Graphite wasn't going to send him there. How could he?

It meant I was on borrowed time though. If Patches didn't present me to the Council, then someone soon would. I was more grateful for Sahara's offer than ever before.

I thanked Patches for the free pass and continued on my way. I headed to my human's garden. I knew that I'd have to take the long route. Otherwise, I'd be caught off-guard.

Curly waited for me on my human's land. I saw him straight away, so at least my legs were saved.

"One Fang was taken to the vets. Graphite is expecting you," Curly said.

Curly was much more optimistic than me. He suspected that he wasn't going to place me on a locked-in order, but I wasn't so sure. He had all of the means to do it now and had

165

to do it for One Fang. He had to have made him a member of the Council immediately.

Stripes saw me and made her way across. It was unusual for her to do that. The news must be urgent. She wasn't anyone's messenger. She agreed with Curly that I might've been too defensive. They'd sought out most of the cats in the Neighbourhood, to tell them their new role. Every cat had their same role, but they worked for the Council. That meant that none of us were allowed to leave the Neighbourhood unless in a car. For most cats, it didn't affect them, and they usually stayed around. They only left when their humans went on holiday or they had to make a visit to the vets. Of course, he had rethought the boundary lines, to no longer include the field. It was a clever way of isolating Sahara.

It was borderline tormenting. Graphite knew that Sahara would be looking down and seeing the Neighbourhood, but no cats would be able to inform her of any of the changes that he'd made. She would have to step into the Neighbourhood and she would be monitored at all times – that was if he didn't expel her from the Neighbourhood altogether.

Dolly and Full Moon were already disbarred from the Cat Council. Graphite summoned them. It was humiliating enough for a member to be disbarred, but to summon them as well was despicable. Graphite must've known that they were staying away as well. They had no way of contacting Sahara because of the new boundaries that he'd set in place. He was really making his mark on the place.

As Stripes and Curly filled me in on what had happened, I got myself comfortable. How had the whole Neighbourhood changed in so little time? I assumed that Graphite had spent a long time thinking about what he was going to do when he took power. I saw a brown tail from the corner of my eye. I knew that it was Autumn.

"Graphite is expecting you," she said.

I had a lot of time for Autumn. I saw that she didn't respect all of these things that Graphite was doing. She must've been to see a whole load of cats already, who he'd been expecting. It would have been a lot quicker to call a whole Neighbourhood meeting. This was a waste of time.

I thanked Autumn for coming for me. I didn't want to be summoned – that wasn't a good feeling. I knew that, and said my goodbyes.

"Why is he having so many meetings?" I asked.

Autumn shrugged her shoulders. I was sure she had an idea, but she wasn't at liberty to discuss what she thought. I could tell by the way that she rolled her eyes that she thought it was a new level of ridiculousness.

I asked whether she'd managed to speak to Sahara to warn her of the new boundaries. She never replied, but the twinkle in her eye told me that she'd found a way. I understood why she didn't say anything to me. It was scary to know that his watchers sat on every corner, and his whisperers were always lurking somewhere near. It was constant surveillance, all of the time.

Autumn took me to Graphite's land though I expected we would've headed to Skinny's. It wasn't as impressive as I thought it would be. The house was large, but the outside was tiny. There was barely enough room to walk around the outside of the property. There was a slither of a path at the front, next to a flower pot. It was disappointing, to say the least. I hoped that he hadn't hosted all of his meetings there. It was an embarrassment.

Graphite kept me waiting for a long time. I started to get bored. I thought about heading home. That was the only good thing about a locked-in order; it meant that I could sleep. I was starting to feel a little lethargic. I sensed a ten-hour nap calling me.

"Inspector White Tip, thank you for stopping by," he said.

I wasn't about to greet him. He was rude enough to have me waiting, so I was rude enough not to talk and bow my head.

"I'm sure that you've been informed of the new boundary lines. Yours are limited. I've spoken with One Fang and I'll be reasonable. As he wasn't a member of the Council before the attack, I won't place you under a locked-in order. However, you're forbidden to cross the road. You may stick to one side, and one side only. Should you break that boundary, I won't hesitate to place you on a permanent locked-in order," Graphite said.

I had no idea what that meant as far as my role within the Neighbourhood. As far as I was concerned, I was still investigating Skinny's disappearance. However, it was going to be a lot more difficult than it had been.

It also meant that I was still able to talk to Dolly and Full Moon. They were still on my side of the road. Of course, it meant that I lost my eight o'clock cuddles. That hurt me. The boy was going to be upset. He'd confided in me a lot. I knew that he was bullied at school and felt like he had no friends except for me. I wasn't going to be around to hear his worries anymore, and I had no way of explaining that to him. That made me feel like the worst cat in the world.

But I didn't argue because I knew better than to argue with Graphite. He could've taken away all of my freedom, which would've been miserable. I gave a single nod to show that I understood and was grateful when he dismissed me. It felt like I'd lost a life. I didn't want him to have the glory of witnessing it.

# 29

## POWERLESS

Even the short distance from Graphite's to my home, I felt like a thousand eyes were watching my every move. It was uncomfortable, to say the least. What had it come to that now the Council would be informed of every cat's every move? It was miserable!

My only saving grace was that the Duchess was home when I got back. I stood on my paws and knocked at the letterbox slowly. She probably thought that she had a human visitor. I sat on the mat, waiting for her to answer the door, looking glumly across the street. If I could've spoken human words, I would've explained to what was happening with my eight o'clock. That was far better than making him think that I'd abandoned him, and he had no friends.

The Duchess opened the door. I trotted past and grabbed a snack in the kitchen. It'd be tough to miss out on food without my eight o'clock cuddles. I didn't want to waste away and made sure that I let out another meow, so that she'd top up my bowl with more, but she didn't understand me. All there was left to do was go to sleep.

When I awoke, the last cat I expected to see was on my land – One Fang! I was seething and furious that he stood on my human's land. It was a step too far.

"I've never seen that cat before," the Male One said.

There was a reason for that. One Fang was supposed to stick to his land. I knew that he'd gone to the vets. He couldn't have been in a good state – he'd lost his tooth. At least he wasn't going to bite me, but it was still a cheek.

The Male One took ages finding a key to let me out. It only made me angrier. My adrenaline pumped. One Fang's eyes were wide. His head leaned back slowly. I knew that he wanted to run. There was no way that he wanted to be there.

"I need your help," One Fang blurted out.

His mouth looked sore. I wondered whether he'd had to have stitches. I thought I'd heard it wrong. One Fang had come to me for help? That was so wrong. It made me feel uncomfortable. We were sworn enemies. That was just how we were.

One Fang explained that he had come to me as a last resort. That made me feel a little more reassured. He'd thought about every cat that he could, but I was the only one he knew who would be able to handle the enormity of the task that he had for me. I wasn't persuaded by flattery, but in the case of facts, I was.

One Fang had told Graphite that I'd attacked him because he was ashamed that he had tripped over the garden hose. He didn't want to be fired. He'd worked hard to get Skinny's land, and Graphite knew that. Graphite had him observe Skinny's land night and day to stop any cat getting it – including Skinny.

"White Tip, I've only been having eight hours of sleep a day," he said.

Eight hours – that was low for a cat. Cats need eighteen hours of sleep. That in itself was enough to make any cat make mistakes.

"You're going to have to give that land up," I warned.

One Fang didn't want to hear it. He'd fought for that land, he said. Skinny didn't deserve it. He'd have done anything, including give up his own human's land for it.

"He can have any land that he wants," One Fang protested, "including your land across the street. You won't be able to use it now. Why does he have to live there?"

"That is Skinny's human home. The human *chose* him. You know what he went through. He should not have to give up that land," I hissed.

"Why did he go there? I had the land sorted. I kept the bird numbers low. He could've gone anywhere," One Fang hissed back.

I supposed it was true. It was One Fang's land to begin with, but Skinny didn't know that. One Fang had several properties, and he went back and forth between them. He claimed he wasn't on the property for a couple of days, and then the human chose Skinny, and let him stay.

It was unfortunate, but if One Fang loved it so much, he shouldn't have left it for so long. I didn't believe that it was only for a couple of days. Birds were much smarter than that. They flew over to check for safe locations. They would've done it for at least a week before choosing to build a nest there. Skinny's human was grateful when Skinny came along. He thought that the garden was overrun with birds. That meant that One Fang had to have left it for a period of weeks. I wasn't about to empathise with a cat who had lost territory that they didn't protect. He only wanted that land when he knew that he could no longer have it. It was ridiculous.

"You had lots of land. Why that one?" I said.

One Fang said it was the best land. I assumed it was because it was the middle house. Cats tend to like middle houses because it means that they can expand their land on either side. An end house was okay, but cats wanted to know that they could walk along the entirety of their land without hassle, without being stopped.

I couldn't understand why One Fang chose to build territory across the road from his human's property. Most cats chose to build it next to their central human home.

One Fang had a good point. He could keep his eye on the property from across the road because he had a better view. He gave Shadows the land because he knew that he'd be able to use it when he needed to, without having to have a fight. It made a lot of sense. He was a terrible fighter, so he had to lessen the chance of having one. It was a good idea.

When he knew about the Skittle Twins being runners, he admitted that he knew that it was easy. They'd often been that way. Sometimes, they'd jump at the sight of a bird, or a leaf blowing off the tree. They were really jumpy. He decided not to take their land from them, but he built up an agreement that he wouldn't attack them, if they allowed him to come and go through their land when he needed to.

I had to commend One Fang. He had quite the operation with Shadows, the Skittle Twins, and Two Prints watching from outside. He knew they weren't the best informers, but they were never going to fight him. The whole time, all of the land belonged to him. It was genius really. I didn't want to operate in that way. I liked my whisperer and watcher to rightly have their own territory, without the constant fear that I could take it away from them whenever I wanted.

"Graphite doesn't want to work with any of them. He believes that the power should be with the top cats, cats in the Cat Council," One Fang said. "He's destroying everything that I have."

It was interesting to see that One Fang would change his stance when there was a threat to his land. He'd betray other cats, so long as he got what he wanted. It was hardly a revelation to know that Graphite wanted land divided up for him and the other members of the Council. That was why they let things slide. They were in full support of his power play. They could own the land without having to fight.

What did it mean for the rest of the cats? Were we supposed to give up everything that we'd worked for? It wasn't fair. No wonder Patches refused to work for him. Who wanted to be a part of the Neighbourhood when there was nothing for them? Cats wanted things for themselves, which was expected. Most cats knew that it was impossible to have the entire Neighbourhood. The humans wouldn't allow it.

Humans could be very ignorant to a lot of things, but not when it affected themselves. Cats were a part of them, so if their cats were wronged, they'd do something about it. No human wanted a tonne of cats on their property that had nothing to do with them.

One Fang might've thought that he owned Shadows' land, but he didn't. She owned it. The humans had chosen her. They put up posters to show that they missed her and wanted her back.

Skinny's human had taken Skinny to the vet when he was hurt. He made sure that only Skinny was on his land, even going so far as to use a hose on cats that he felt were intruding.

My humans were also fierce and protective. I knew that there was no way that they would allow other cats to take ownership of the land. The Male One let me chase off any cats away that I didn't want. The Duchess, although she shouldn't have, sometimes she fed my friends. She actively encouraged them to come to see me. I didn't want her to, because it was my food that they were eating. They knew the difference between my friends and foes. I couldn't see how Graphite was going to ensure that cats of the Council had the amount of land that he promised them.

There were also the humans that had dogs living with them. Some of those humans really hated cats. They allowed their dogs to chase cats off their land. Were they going to allow members of the Council to have a part of their land – no.

One Fang was right to be worried. I would've been concerned too, and I was. I'd already lost my eight o'clock cuddles, but that was just one property. One Fang had lost the same amount, but he was supposed to be working with Graphite.

"Why has he allowed you to come here today?" I asked.

I knew that Graphite wanted to know where every cat was and what every cat was doing. It was the only way that he was able to monitor who went across the boundaries. I firmly believed now that he wanted to cut Sahara off and punish her.

"He thinks I've come to tell you that you are confined to this land only, and he knew that it'd take some time to deliver the news," he said.

One Fang was unbelievable. That was absolutely what he was doing. What choice did I have? I was losing my land. One Fang delivered the message to me that I was losing my land, which I knew Graphite would love. That was why he agreed to it in the first place.

"Whatever help you think I can give you, you're wrong. I won't be helping you with anything," I hissed.

How dare he think that I would let him off for this? One Fang probably took great pleasure in knowing that he was going to take the land away from me. I was his sworn enemy. I should've seen it coming. Whatever he wanted to do to Graphite, I wasn't interested.

To think that I'd given him any of my time! It was unbelievable. I chased him off my land before he decided that he had any more news to tell me.

# 30

## PUSHING THE BOUNDARIES

Stripes thought that I'd reacted too soon. She thought I should've seen who was receiving the land first before I told One Fang to leave. I don't know what difference it would've made. I knew I was going to see the new owner within a matter of days, if I was lucky. Graphite was working at the speed of light. They were probably already there.

It was another way of forcing me onto the street, so that Graphite knew where I was going and who I was speaking to. The restricted boundaries I had meant that I had to wait for Curly to talk to me. I wasn't even able to talk with my whisperer, unless he came to speak to me.

"Who would be the worst cat to take over?" Curly said.

I thought Graphite or One Fang were terrible choices. I wasn't sure that I was able to stomach either of them occupying the land next to me. Then, as Curly always does, he made me realise that there were even worse choices.

"Pomeranian's Friend," he laughed.

I didn't find it as funny. There was no way that I was going to fight with Pomeranian's Friend. I was pretty sure that the humans would have pest control in to get rid of him.

Maybe Graphite expected for me to feel lucky because he hadn't placed an official locked-in order on me. My freedom was disappearing through my paws.

"Seriously, what do you think that One Fang was asking you?" Stripes said.

I supposed that One Fang wanted me to find a way to get his land back and maybe his whisperer. There was no way that Skippy was going to work for him again willingly. Shadows might've been easier to persuade. She was still feeling heartbroken that she'd been dismissed. I think she would've been grateful to be working for One Fang again.

"As if you'd work for him, when he stole Skinny's land," Stripes growled.

I knew that Stripes hated One Fang. It wasn't enough to offer Skinny other land and other humans. He deserved to be with his humans. They cared about him after all. There was no way that Stripes was ever going to even consider working with him again.

Curly thought it was good that cracks were starting to show between One Fang and Graphite. If One Fang thought he was going too far, that meant he was willing to act soon.

"I think he spoke to you because he wanted to test whether you would act with him," Curly said.

It did sound plausible. One Fang knew that I'd want to get my land back. I would've fought hard to make sure that I didn't have to give it up, but I wouldn't work with him. I couldn't.

Curly was far more objective than either Stripes or I could be. He believed that One Fang had to be desperate. He was right. One by one, Graphite had removed the cats that he was used to relying on. He wanted to make sure that I was going into the Neighbourhood. He wanted some of Graphite's buttons pushed. Curly worked it out that when I stuck to my side of the street, that I was able to keep to it and still end up at Skinny's land.

Crescent Drive wrapped around to join Perigee Close. This looped around in a U shape to join back with Crescent Drive. I was still able to roam the Neighbourhood without breaking any of my restrictions. There was also no official block break from this side of the street. It was genius. It didn't help me to get to either my eight o'clock cuddles or onto Curly's land, but it widened the area.

I knew that Graphite would be furious when he realised that I'd taken him so literally. If he restricted me anymore, then it'd be known as unreasonable. Other cats within the Council wouldn't defend me, but it meant that I could get to Skinny's land.

Once Stripes and Curly left, I asked them to make it obvious that they were leaving my land. I needed them to act as a distraction for me. I decided that I'd use the fence tops first. I knew that the watchers would have to be on the other sides of their roofs. I comfortably got three-quarters of the way without being seen by another cat. Curly made sure that he and Stripes sat in the middle of the road having a conversation. They appeared to be describing a fight. He could be a great actor when he needed to be.

The cat that I most needed to avoid was Jet. Jet lived on Perigee Close. She'd no doubt have spotted me, if it wasn't for Curly and Stripes. There was a little break in the fence, so I had to walk to the front of the land, and then I went around the back of the land.

When I saw One Fang wasn't there. I jumped down into Skinny's land I looked at the sparrows again. I sat watching them for a while, and I waited to pounce. When suddenly, a voice said, "Back off, White Tip, those sparrows are mine."

I would've been seriously angry about losing out on a hunt if it hadn't been Skinny Hind.

# 31

## A NEAR MISS

Skinny had lost a bit of weight since I'd last seen him. He'd been shaved a lot. There was hardly any long fur on him. I could see that he'd been through a lot. It was understandable that he looked worse for wear.

When Skinny explained that he was set upon by Graphite, I felt angry. He was lay sleeping on his back in the garden when he felt a pain to his whole body. He opened his eyes to find Graphite standing on top of him. Graphite was a substantial cat. He was stocky and well-fed. I imagined that it would've been painful for Skinny, who was a lot smaller than him. Skinny started to lose breath when Graphite jumped off and rolled him over. He bit into his shoulder and scratched like crazy. Skinny said that he had no idea which direction he'd go next.

Next, a black cat ran past and shoved him into the pond. When he came back for air, Graphite stood on his neck. He only stepped off when Skinny stopped fighting back.

The next thing he could remember was his human crying and carrying him under a blanket to his car. He had to spend a long time at the vets because he had abscesses. The vet transferred him to a special vet, so that he could have an operation and receive vital fluids. Skinny didn't know why. Then, he wasn't allowed to go outside for a while.

Skinny saw One Fang and Graphite hanging around the land and wondered what they were doing there. When I explained that One Fang had taken over the land, Skinny looked worried for a minute.

"Does One Fang know that you're back?" I asked.

"I don't think so. This is the first time that I've been able to go outside," Skinny said.

It'd be better if One Fang didn't know that Skinny was back. Skinny needed rest. One Fang was in a good enough condition that he could take Skinny on and probably cause more damage. Skinny wasn't having any of it. I understood that. He'd been cooped up inside for a long time. He was probably excited to get some fresh air.

I was pleasantly surprised when Curly made his appearance. He managed to convince Two Prints not to say a word. I don't think Two Prints would've done unless they pestered him. Curly agreed to be on the land for when One Fang came back. It worried me. I wanted Curly to have total freedom. As a whisperer, he needed to be able to tell me what was happening in the Neighbourhood. Stripes was good, but she couldn't hear what was happening because she was up high, away from the conversation.

Curly was right. I needed to leave the land as soon as possible and make my way back home. The longer I was there, the more likely it was that one of Graphite's informants would spot me and inform him that I was there. I didn't want to lose more land. If I lost my human land, which was possible with him, I'd be totally miserable.

I tiptoed across the tops of the fences. It was difficult to use feather paws for so long. I had to keep shifting my weight. As a larger cat, it made it tricky. Feather paws was usually much easier for a kitten or a more petite adult.

Jet's tail caught the corner of my eye, I very nearly got caught. The tail swished from left to right, meaning that something had caught her eye. Fortunately, she had her back to me. Otherwise, I knew that she would've seen me. I leaned back as far as I could without falling off the fence and giving myself away.

I tried my best to take a sneak peek at what Jet was eying up. One Fang trotted across the street. There was no other cat, so it had to be him. Did that mean that she didn't like him? I wasn't sure that she trusted him.

Jet glided down from the bonnet of the car. She was so graceful; I doubt she would've made a sound as she landed. She crept towards One Fang. She didn't trust him! One Fang froze. He leaned on three paws. That meant that he wasn't expecting to be caught.

Whilst Jet questioned One Fang, I took my opportunity to sneak past and head back towards home before she could see me. I was careful to make sure that I maintained feather paws as I tiptoed along the fence.

I was on my line of the street, two houses from home, when I felt the fence shake beneath my feet. That could only mean one thing. There was a cat on the fence with me. I turned my head back, just enough, so that I could keep my balance.

"Inspector White Tip, have you been exploring?" Autumn whispered.

I carried on until I got to my land. Autumn worked for Graphite. I wasn't about to tell her everything. She could be discreet and was a good informant for a listener. The problem was that I had no idea where her loyalties lay. I assumed that she had obligations to inform Graphite of everything.

Autumn followed me when I jumped down to my land. I hadn't expected her to follow me, but she did. She landed silently. I wanted to know how she did that. It seemed to be something that cats within the Council were able to do. It was a skill that I'd never learned, but I would've liked to have known.

"Can you be here?" I asked.

Autumn walked with her head held high. She could walk anywhere that she wanted to. She was an informant. There were fewer rules on her. She didn't have to tell Graphite everything; she could filter some of it. Graphite assumed that she was doing something for the better of the Council, even when she wasn't.

I told her that she had to be careful. I suspected that Graphite wouldn't always be so trusting. He had shown that he didn't trust many of the cats. He'd turn on her at some point. He'd have her traced.

"Cats like him are dangerous," I warned. "You don't want to be caught out by your own complacency."

Autumn appeared to be offended. I knew that she was a very capable cat, which was why I didn't want to see her being caught. She didn't deserve that. She needed to be free to walk across the land.

"Graphite isn't as powerful as he likes cats to believe. He's told cats that they have to tell him everything, but none of them really respect him. How can he know that they're being honest?" Autumn asked.

"Jet seems to be very compliant. I saw her chase down One Fang today," I said.

"Jet thinks that he'll make her his deputy. She has to show that she's compliant and holding up the rules," Autumn said.

Autumn wasn't supposed to be telling me any of that. She was obligated to only speak with Graphite about what she knew. She knew that some of the cats did as they pleased. They didn't tell Graphite everything.

"I saw you on Skinny's land. I'm glad that he's well," she admitted.

Where had she been? Autumn was such an inconspicuous cat! I'd done my best not to be seen, yet she'd seen me. I worried that there might have been others, but she reassured me that she was the only one. The rest of the cats were distracted by Stripes and Curly, or sleeping.

"He deserves to have his land back," I said.

"I agree," Autumn said with a smile. "I'm not going to say anything. I don't want to know what Graphite would do if he saw him."

Autumn admitted to knowing what happened to Skinny. She also knew about Jet. Dolly had told her.

"Curly is there in case they come back," I explained.

Autumn agreed that Curly needed to be there for protection. One Fang might not attack him, but Graphite would. Curly was a good fighter.

"Won't he be placed under a locked-in order?" Autumn asked.

"He could, but then he'd have to go to the Stables. Curly has no inside land," I explained.

I wanted Graphite to discover Curly. It was our only chance of communicating with Sahara.

# 32

## GRAPHITE'S SCARS

Curly made sure that Jet had seen him, as he headed over to Skinny Hind's land. He was such a clever cat. He knew how everything was going to happen, detail by detail.

Jet waited until Curly was out of sight. Then, when she saw One Fang, she made sure to inform him that she saw Curly. That was why her tail swished. It was because she needed to pass on tuna. She was just as angry as Graphite. One Fang ran back to tell Graphite what had happened. Graphite headed straight over to Skinny Hind's land.

Graphite knew that Curly was much better at fighting than he was. He sent Skinny inside before Graphite arrived. He didn't need to get caught up in the cat fight. If anything, he needed to stay as far away as possible. I wasn't sure he'd recover after the last time.

Curly made sure that he sat in the corner of the garden, shaded by the tree, with the sparrows above. I was surprised that they didn't fly away until they saw Graphite. As soon as they saw him, they flew away. Curly said that he remained calm.

Graphite walked closer. He was so caught up in his anger, that he never made sure that he had back up when he ran over. Curly claimed that he never bothered walking circles because he didn't want any of the other cats coming close, taking him by surprise. Instead, he ran forward at him.

Graphite expected that Curly would offer him more respect. I've no idea why he thought that. Graphite didn't know what to do. He stayed rooted to the spot, almost too afraid to remain on the land. Who knew that he was a runner when he had the choice?

Curly never told me what happened after that. I saw for myself that Graphite had come away with the worst. He had three claws marks that spanned across his entire face. He never told anyone, but I think he was secretly pleased that they made him look more intimidating. Curly had a few words with Graphite. He made sure that Graphite restored the land back to Skinny.

I was surprised that Graphite gave up One Fang's land. He seemed to have worked so hard for it. One Fang trusted in him. Graphite had wound him up so much about making sure that he guarded the land; that it had to have been gutting to hear that it was no longer his.

Stripes came down to tell me that she saw Graphite heading over to Skinny's land. I knew that the other cats would have seen this. The watchers would've seen him doing this, after they saw Curly over there. I knew that it was safe to head over there. Even if it wasn't, I didn't care. I wanted to support Curly.

Jet guarded the front of Skinny's property. Her eyes narrowed when she saw me. She was used to cats doing what she told them. She hid behind her duties for the Council. Had she have been operating for the Council, I would've stayed away, but it was only for Graphite. Without Ebony, the best she could do was try to fight me. There was no way that she was going to do that.

I ran to Shadows' land. The best way to get onto Skinny's land was that way. Curly would get a better view of me from the top of the fence than the gate at the side of the house.

I didn't want to shock him. I wanted him to fight Graphite and win.

Shadows was a little shocked when she saw me, but she wasn't going to fight me. She was grateful that I'd convinced her to go home.

"Close to the fence, as close as you can get. Slow jump. Front paws first," Shadows whispered.

I knew how to jump onto a fence. I'd jumped onto many fences. Though I had never done it quite like that, but I still gave it a go. My back legs absorbed the shock, but the land was silent. I made a note to make sure that she taught me how to do that on a descend jump.

By the time I got there, Graphite had left, and Curly was nowhere to be seen. The garden was eerily quiet. I only heard the birds in the tree, which meant that both of them had to have left long before I got there. It didn't matter how loud I was on the landing. I jumped down. I didn't really care for walking on the tops of fences if I didn't have to. It was uncomfortable, and the fence panel was always shaky underfoot.

As soon as I landed, I felt something swipe at my leg – Curly Whiskers. He was flawless, for now.

I was only sad that I didn't take Graphite for myself.

"You know that they're coming for you don't you?" I acknowledged.

"Yeah, but when they do, I'm going to make sure that it's worth my while." Curly shrugged as he leapt over the fence onto the field.

# ABOUT THE AUTHOR

Sophie Eden is a wife and a mum. She studied Law at the University of Salford. After travelling in Canada, she returned home and after three years, trained as a primary teacher.

In 2016, Sophie adopted her black and white cat, Oscar. He was in a sorry state as he lay there, with overgrown claws. He was the only cat silent and not bothering to try and gain the human's attention. As she unhooked his claws from the crate, her husband decided that they had to adopt that one. The only history that they were given was that he had been a stray for six months, and had been fond of the family's little boy, but he fought continuously with their other two cats, so they brought him to the animal shelter.

When Oscar came home, he meowed in appreciation and then hid behind the sofa for most of the evening. Then the next night, Oscar escaped out of the garden. Two nights later, Oscar was spotted on the roof of a neighbour's house. Sophie's husband, David, picked him up and carried him home, his hands bleeding from the scratches. As soon as he saw Sophie, he purred. Oscar has remained loyal to them ever since. When the Little Lady arrived, Oscar would often sleep under her Moses basket to keep her safe. Now, he purrs when she offers him cuddles, but keeps a close eye for where she might be.

Oscar had some very fierce land fights with a ginger and white cat, who Sophie and David named Old Ginger Paws. After falling in a pond, he was taken to the vets because he was very ill, and had to have surgery. Strangely, the ginger and white cat has never been seen again, which was where the idea of runners came from.

It seemed as though he hated other cats, until three years later, a striped tabby cat came looking for some food. She was shy and jumpy. A couple of times, Oscar chased her off the land, but he never fought her. Sophie and David would feed her, and Oscar seemed to look out for her. She shows up once in a while, when she wants some food, and the pair of them sit in the garden together, but no other cats are welcome. He has made quite the impression with people in the neighbourhood, who often ask about his whereabouts and feed him, which was where the idea of the eight o' clock cuddles came from.

To find out more about Inspector White Tip, check out his website www.inspectorwhitetip.com.